The Snow Queen

The Snow Queen

And Other Stories

OSCAR WILDE
BROTHERS GRIMM
HANS CHRISTIAN ANDERSEN

Vitasta

Published by
Renu Kaul Verma
Vitasta Publishing Pvt Ltd
4348/4C, Ansari Road, Daryaganj
New Delhi - 110 002
info@vitastapublishing.com

ISBN: 978-81-19670-67-3

First Edition 2025

MRP ₹ 295

We gratefully acknowledge Project Gutenberg, for making this book possible.

Layout & Cover Design by Shubhpreet Kaur
Printed at Chaman Enterprises, New Delhi

The value of fairy tales lies not in a brief literary escape from reality, but in the gift of hope that goodness truly is more powerful than evil and that even the darkest reality can lead to a happy ending.

-Alane Ferguson

Contents

Publisher's Note

In this enchanting collection, we present a carefully curated selection of timeless tales from two masters of the fairy tale tradition: the Brothers Grimm and Hans Christian Andersen. These stories have captivated readers for generations, weaving magic and moral lessons into narratives that continue to resonate with both children and adults alike.

The Brothers Grimm, Jacob and Wilhelm, travelled across German-speaking regions in the early nineteenth century, collecting and preserving folk tales that might otherwise have been lost to time. Their work stands as a cultural treasure, capturing the essence of oral storytelling traditions whilst exploring universal themes of courage, kindness, and the triumph of good over evil.

Hans Christian Andersen, the Danish literary genius, brought his own distinct sensibility to the fairy tale form. Drawing from folklore but infusing stories with his unique perspective, Andersen created tales of remarkable depth and emotional resonance that often speak directly to the complexities of the human condition.

This volume brings together beloved classics from both traditions: the cautionary brilliance of *The Red Shoes,* the clever twists of *Rumpelstiltskin,* the enduring hope found in *Cinderella,* the wintry adventure of *The Snow Queen,* and the brave siblings of *Hansel and Gretel,* among others. Each tale has been faithfully presented to preserve the authentic voice of its creator whilst ensuring accessibility for contemporary readers.

Whether you are discovering these stories for the first time or revisiting cherished childhood memories, we invite you to lose yourself in these magical worlds. Like all great literature, these tales merit repeated readings, revealing new layers of meaning as we journey through different stages of life.

THE RED SHOES

Hans Christian Andersen

Once upon a time there was little girl, pretty and dainty. But in summer time she was obliged to go barefooted because she was poor, and in winter she had to wear large wooden shoes, so that her little instep grew quite red.

In the middle of the village lived an old shoemaker's wife; she sat down and made, as well as she could, a pair of little shoes out of some old pieces of red cloth. They were clumsy, but she meant well, for they were intended for the little girl, whose name was Karen.

Karen received the shoes and wore them for the first time on the day of her mother's funeral. They were certainly not suitable for mourning; but she had no others, and so she put her bare feet into them and walked behind the humble coffin.

Just then a large old carriage came by, and in it sat an

old lady; she looked at the little girl, and taking pity on her, said to the clergyman, 'Look here, if you will give me the little girl, I will take care of her.'

Karen believed that this was all on account of the red shoes, but the old lady thought them hideous, and so they were burnt. Karen herself was dressed very neatly and cleanly; she was taught to read and to sew, and people said that she was pretty. But the mirror told her, 'You are more than pretty—you are beautiful.'

One day, the Queen was travelling through that part of the country, and had her little daughter, who was a princess, with her. All the people, amongst them Karen too, streamed towards the castle, where the little princess, in fine white clothes, stood before the window and allowed herself to be stared at. She wore neither a train nor a golden crown, but beautiful red morocco shoes; they were indeed much finer than those which the shoemaker's wife had sewn for little Karen. There is really nothing in the world that can be compared to red shoes!

Karen was now old enough to be confirmed; she received some new clothes, and she was also to have some new shoes. The rich shoemaker in the town took the measure of her little foot in his own room, in which there stood great glass cases full of pretty shoes and white slippers. It all looked very lovely, but the old lady could not see very well, and therefore did not get much pleasure out of it. Amongst the shoes stood a pair of red ones, like those which the princess had worn. How beautiful they were! And the shoemaker said that they had been made for a count's daughter, but that they had not fitted her.

'I suppose they are of shiny leather?' asked the old lady. 'They shine so.'

'Yes, they do shine,' said Karen. They fitted her, and were bought. But the old lady knew nothing of their being red, for she would never have allowed Karen to be confirmed in red shoes, as she was now to be.

Everybody looked at her feet, and the whole of the way from the church door to the choir it seemed to her as if even the ancient figures on the monuments, in their stiff collars and long black robes, had their eyes fixed on her red shoes. It was only of these that she thought when the clergyman laid his hand upon her head and spoke of the holy baptism, of the covenant with God, and told her that she was now to be a grown-up Christian. The organ pealed forth solemnly, and the sweet children's voices mingled with that of their old leader; but Karen thought only of her red shoes. In the afternoon the old lady heard from everybody that Karen had worn red shoes. She said that it was a shocking thing to do, that it was very improper, and that Karen was always to go to church in future in black shoes, even if they were old.

On the following Sunday, there was Communion. Karen looked first at the black shoes, then at the red ones—looked at the red ones again, and put them on.

The sun was shining gloriously, so Karen and the old lady went along the footpath through the corn, where it was rather dusty.

At the church door stood an old crippled soldier

leaning on a crutch; he had a wonderfully long beard, more red than white, and he bowed down to the ground and asked the old lady whether he might wipe her shoes. Then Karen put out her little foot too. 'Dear me, what pretty dancing-shoes!' said the soldier. 'Sit fast, when you dance,' said he, addressing the shoes, and slapping the soles with his hand.

The old lady gave the soldier some money and then went with Karen into the church.

And all the people inside looked at Karen's red shoes, and all the figures gazed at them; when Karen knelt before the altar and put the golden goblet to her mouth, she thought only of the red shoes. It seemed to her as though they were swimming about in the goblet, and she forgot to sing the psalm, forgot to say the 'Lord's Prayer.'

Now everyone came out of church, and the old lady stepped into her carriage. But just as Karen was lifting up her foot to get in too, the old soldier said: 'Dear me, what pretty dancing shoes!' and Karen could not help it, she was obliged to dance a few steps; and when she had once begun, her legs continued to dance. It seemed as if the shoes had got power over them. She danced round the church corner, for she could not stop; the coachman had to run after her and seize her. He lifted her into the carriage, but her feet continued to dance, so that she kicked the good old lady violently. At last they took off her shoes, and her legs were at rest.

At home the shoes were put into the cupboard, but Karen could not help looking at them.

Now the old lady fell ill, and it was said that she would not rise from her bed again. She had to be nursed and waited upon, and this was no one's duty more than Karen's. But there was a grand ball in the town, and Karen was invited. She looked at the red shoes, saying to herself that there was no sin in doing that; she put the red shoes on, thinking there was no harm in that either; and then she went to the ball; and commenced to dance.

But when she wanted to go to the right, the shoes danced to the left, and when she wanted to dance up the room, the shoes danced down the room, down the stairs through the street, and out through the gates of the town. She danced, and was obliged to dance, far out into the dark wood. Suddenly something shone up among the trees, and she believed it was the moon, for it was a face. But it was the old soldier with the red beard; he sat there nodding his head and said: 'Dear me, what pretty dancing shoes!'

She was frightened, and wanted to throw the red shoes away; but they stuck fast. She tore off her stockings, but the shoes had grown fast to her feet. She danced and was obliged to go on dancing over field and meadow, in rain and sunshine, by night and by day—but by night it was most horrible.

She danced out into the open churchyard; but the dead there did not dance. They had something better to do than that. She wanted to sit down on the pauper's grave where the bitter fern grows; but for her there was neither peace nor rest. And as she danced past the open church door she saw an angel there in long white robes, with wings reaching from his shoulders down to the earth; his face was stern and grave, and in his hand he held a broad shining sword.

'Dance you shall,' said he, 'dance in your red shoes till you are pale and cold, till your skin shrivels up and you are a skeleton! Dance you shall, from door to door, and where proud and wicked children live you shall knock, so that they may hear you and fear you! Dance you shall, dance—!'

'Mercy!' cried Karen. But she did not hear what the angel answered, for the shoes carried her through the gate into the fields, along highways and byways, and unceasingly she had to dance.

One morning she danced past a door that she knew well; they were singing a psalm inside, and a coffin was being carried out covered with flowers. Then she knew that she was forsaken by everyone and damned by the angel of God.

She danced, and was obliged to go on dancing through the dark night. The shoes bore her away over thorns and stumps till she was all torn and bleeding; she danced away over the heath to a lonely little house. Here, she knew, lived the executioner; and she tapped with her finger at the window and said:

'Come out, come out! I cannot come in, for I must dance.'

And the executioner said, 'I don't suppose you know who I am. I strike off the heads of the wicked, and I notice that my axe is tingling to do so.'

'Don't cut off my head!' said Karen, 'for then I could not repent of my sin. But cut off my feet with the red shoes.'

And then she confessed all her sin, and the executioner struck off her feet with the red shoes; but the shoes danced away with the little feet across the field into the deep forest.

And he carved her a pair of wooden feet and some crutches, and taught her a psalm which is always sung by sinners; she kissed the hand that guided the axe, and went away over the heath.

'Now, I have suffered enough for the red shoes,' she said; 'I will go to church, so that people can see me.' And she went quickly up to the church-door; but when she came there, the red shoes were dancing before her, and she was frightened, and turned back.

During the whole week she was sad and wept many bitter tears, but when Sunday came again she said: 'Now I have suffered and striven enough. I believe I am quite as good as many of those who sit in church and give themselves airs.' And so she went boldly on; but she had not got farther than the churchyard gate when she saw the red shoes dancing along before her. Then she became terrified, and turned back and repented right heartily of her sin.

She went to the parsonage, and begged that she might be taken into service there. She would be industrious, she said, and do everything that she could; she did not mind about the wages as long as she had a roof over her, and was with good people. The pastor's wife had pity on her, and took her into service. And she was industrious and thoughtful. She sat quiet and listened when the pastor read aloud from the Bible in the evening. All the children liked her very much, but when they spoke about dress and grandeur and beauty, she would shake her head.

On the following Sunday they all went to church, and she was asked whether she wished to go too; but, with tears in her eyes, she looked sadly at her crutches. And then the others went to hear God's Word, but she went alone into her little room; this was only large enough to hold the bed and a chair. Here she sat down with her hymn-book, and as she was reading it with a pious mind, the wind carried the notes of the organ over to her from the church, and in tears she lifted up her face and said: 'O God! help me!'

Then the sun shone so brightly, and right before her stood an angel of God in white robes; it was the same one whom she had seen that night at the church-door. He no longer carried the sharp sword, but a beautiful green branch, full of roses; with this he touched the ceiling, which rose up very high, and where he had touched it there shone a golden star. He touched the walls, which opened wide apart, and she saw the organ which was pealing forth; she saw the pictures of the old pastors and their wives, and the congregation sitting in the polished chairs and singing from their hymn-books. The church itself had come to the poor girl in her narrow room, or the room had gone to the church. She sat in the pew with the rest of the pastor's household, and when they had finished the hymn and looked up, they nodded and said, 'It was right of you to come, Karen.'

'It was mercy,' said she.

The organ played and the children's voices in the choir sounded soft and lovely. The bright warm sunshine streamed through the window into the pew where Karen sat, and her heart became so filled with it, so filled with peace and joy, that it broke. Her soul flew on the sunbeams to Heaven, and no one was there who asked after the Red Shoes.

RAPUNZEL

Brothers Grimm

There were once a man and a woman who had long in vain wished for a child. At length, the woman hoped that God was about to grant her desire. These people had a little window at the back of their house from which a splendid garden could be seen, which was full of the most beautiful flowers and herbs. It was, however, surrounded by a high wall, and no one dared to go into it because it belonged to an enchantress, who had great power and was dreaded by all the world. One day the woman was standing by this window and looking down into the garden, when she saw a bed which was planted with the most beautiful rampion (rapunzel), and it looked so fresh and green that she longed for it. She quite pined away, and began to look pale and miserable. Then her husband was alarmed, and asked: 'What ails you, dear wife?' 'Ah,' she replied, 'if I can't eat some of the rampion, which is in the garden behind our house, I shall die.' The man, who loved her, thought: 'Sooner than let your wife die, bring her some of the rampion yourself, let it cost what it will.' At twilight, he clambered down over the wall into the garden of the enchantress, hastily clutched a handful of rampion, and took it to his wife. She at once made herself a salad of it, and ate it greedily. It tasted so good to her—so very good, that the next day she longed for it three times as much as before. If he was to have any rest, her husband must once more descend into the garden. In the gloom of evening therefore, he let himself down again; but when he had clambered down the wall he was terribly afraid, for he saw the enchantress standing before him.

'How can you dare,' said she with an angry look, 'descend into my garden and steal my rampion like a thief? You shall suffer for it!'

'Ah,' answered he, 'let mercy take the place of justice, I only made up my mind to do it out of necessity. My wife saw your rampion from the window, and felt such a longing for it that she would have died if she had not got some to eat.'

Then the enchantress allowed her anger to be softened, and said to him: 'If the case be as you say, I will allow you to take away with you as much rampion as you will, only I make one condition, you must give me the child which your wife will bring into the world; it shall be well treated, and I will care for it like a mother.'

The man in his terror consented to everything, and

when the woman was brought to bed, the enchantress appeared at once, gave the child the name of Rapunzel, and took it away with her.

Rapunzel grew into the most beautiful child under the sun. When she was twelve years old, the enchantress shut her into a tower, which lay in a forest, and had neither stairs nor door, but quite at the top was a little window. When the enchantress wanted to go in, she placed herself beneath it and cried:

'Rapunzel, Rapunzel, Let down your hair to me.'

Rapunzel had magnificent long hair, fine as spun gold, and when she heard the voice of the enchantress, she unfastened her braided tresses, wound them round one of the hooks of the window above, and then the hair fell twenty ells down, and the enchantress climbed up by it.

After a year or two, it came to pass that the king's son rode through the forest and passed by the tower. Then he heard a song, which was so charming that he stood still and listened. This was Rapunzel, who in her solitude passed her time in letting her sweet voice resound. The king's son wanted to climb up to her, and looked for the door of the tower, but none was to be found. He rode home, but the singing had so deeply touched his heart, that every day he went out into the forest and listened to it. Once when he was thus standing behind a tree, he saw that an enchantress came there, and he heard how she cried:

'Rapunzel, Rapunzel, Let down your hair to me.'

Then Rapunzel let down the braids of her hair, and

the enchantress climbed up to her. 'If that is the ladder by which one mounts, I too will try my fortune,' said he, and the next day when it began to grow dark, he went to the tower and cried:

'Rapunzel, Rapunzel, Let down your hair to me.'

Immediately the hair fell down and the king's son climbed up.

At first Rapunzel was terribly frightened when a man, such as her eyes had never yet beheld, came to her; but the king's son began to talk to her quite like a friend, and told her that his heart had been so stirred that it had let him have no rest, and he had been forced to see her.

Then Rapunzel lost her fear, and when he asked her if she would take him for her husband, and she saw that he was young and handsome, she thought: He will love me more than old Dame Gothel does; and she said 'yes', and laid her hand in his. She said: 'I will willingly go away with you, but I do not know how to get down. Bring with you a skein of silk every time that you come, and I will weave a ladder with it, and when that is ready I will descend, and you will take me on your horse.'

They agreed that until that time he should come to her every evening, for the old woman came by day. The enchantress remarked nothing of this, until once Rapunzel said to her: 'Tell me, Dame Gothel, how it happens that you are so much heavier for me to draw up than the young king's son—he is with me in a moment.'

'Ah! you wicked child,' cried the enchantress. 'What do I hear you say! I thought I had separated you from all the world, and yet you have deceived me!' In her anger she clutched Rapunzel's beautiful tresses, wrapped them twice round her left hand, seized a pair of scissors with the right, and snip, snap, they were cut off, and the lovely braids lay on the ground. And she was so pitiless that she took poor Rapunzel into a desert where she had to live in great grief and misery.

On the same day that she cast out Rapunzel, however, the enchantress fastened the braids of hair, which she had cut off, to the hook of the window, and when the king's son came and cried:

'Rapunzel, Rapunzel, Let down your hair to me.'

She let the hair down. The king's son ascended, but instead of finding his dearest Rapunzel, he found the enchantress, who gazed at him with wicked and venomous looks. 'Aha!' she cried mockingly, 'you would fetch your dearest, but the beautiful bird sits no longer singing in the nest; the cat has got it, and will scratch out your eyes as well. Rapunzel is lost to you; you will never see her again.'

The king's son was beside himself with pain, and in his despair he leapt down from the tower. He escaped with his life, but the thorns into which he fell pierced his eyes. Then he wandered quite blind about the forest, ate nothing but roots and berries, and did naught but lament and weep over the loss of his dearest wife.

Thus he roamed about in misery for some years, and at length came to the desert where Rapunzel, with the twins to which she had given birth, a boy and a girl, lived in wretchedness. He heard a voice, and it seemed so familiar to him that he went towards it, and when he approached, Rapunzel knew him and fell on his neck and wept. Two of her tears wetted his eyes and they grew clear again, and he could see with them as before. He led her to his kingdom where he was joyfully received, and they lived for a long time afterwards, happy and contented.

THE SELFISH GIANT

Oscar Wilde

Every afternoon, as they were coming from school, the children used to go and play in the Giant's garden.

It was a large, lovely garden, with soft green grass. Here and there over the grass stood beautiful flowers like stars, and there were twelve peach-trees that in the spring-time broke out into delicate blossoms of pink and pearl, and in the autumn bore rich fruit. The birds sat on the trees and sang so sweetly that the children used to stop their games in order to listen to them. 'How happy we are here!' they cried to each other.

One day the Giant came back. He had been to visit his friend the Cornish ogre, and had stayed with him for seven years. After the seven years were over he had said all that he had to say, for his conversation was limited, and he determined to return to his own castle. When he arrived he saw the children playing in the garden.

'What are you doing here?' he cried in a very gruff voice, and the children ran away.

'My own garden is my own garden,' said the Giant; 'any one can understand that, and I will allow nobody to play in it but myself.' So he built a high wall all round it, and put up a notice-board.

TRESPASSERS WILL BE PROSECUTED

He was a very selfish giant.

The poor children had now nowhere to play. They tried to play on the road, but the road was very dusty and full of hard stones, and they did not like it. They used to wander round the high wall when their lessons were over, and talk about the beautiful garden inside. 'How happy we were there,' they said to each other.

Then the Spring came, and all over the country, there were little blossoms and little birds. Only in the garden of the Selfish Giant it was still winter. The birds did not care to sing in it as there were no children, and the trees forgot to blossom. Once a beautiful flower put its head out from the grass, but when it saw the notice-board it was so sorry for the children that it slipped back into the ground again, and went off to sleep.

The only people who were pleased were the Snow and the Frost. 'Spring has forgotten this garden,' they cried, 'so we will live here all the year round.' The Snow covered up the grass with her great white cloak, and the Frost painted all the trees silver.

Then they invited the North Wind to stay with them,

and he came. He was wrapped in furs, and he roared all day about the garden, and blew the chimney-pots down. 'This is a delightful spot,' he said, 'we must ask the Hail on a visit.'

So the Hail came. Every day, for three hours he rattled on the roof of the castle till he broke most of the slates, and then he ran round and round the garden as fast as he could go. He was dressed in grey, and his breath was like ice.

'I cannot understand why the Spring is so late in coming,' said the Selfish Giant, as he sat at the window and looked out at his cold white garden; 'I hope there will be a change in the weather.'

But the Spring never came, nor the Summer. The Autumn gave golden fruit to every garden, but to the Giant's garden she gave none. 'He is too selfish,' she said. So it was always Winter there, and the North Wind, and the Hail, and the Frost, and the Snow danced about through the trees.

One morning, the Giant was lying awake in bed when he heard some lovely music. It sounded so sweet to his ears that he thought it must be the King's musicians passing by.

It was really only a little linnet singing outside his window, but it was so long since he had heard a bird sing in his garden that it seemed to him to be the most beautiful music in the world. Then the Hail stopped dancing over his head, and the North Wind ceased roaring, and a delicious perfume came to him through the open casement. 'I believe the Spring has come at last,' said the Giant; and he jumped out of bed and looked out.

What did he see?

He saw a most wonderful sight. Through a little hole in the wall the children had crept in, and they were sitting in the branches of the trees. In every tree that he could see there was a little child. And the trees were so glad to have the children back again that they had covered themselves with blossoms, and were waving their arms gently above the children's heads. The birds were flying about and twittering with delight, and the flowers were looking up through the green grass and laughing. It was a lovely scene, only in one corner it was still winter. It was the farthest corner of the garden, and in it was standing a little boy. He was so small that he could not reach up to the branches of the tree, and he was wandering all round it, crying bitterly. The poor tree was still quite covered with frost and snow, and the North Wind was blowing and roaring above it. 'Climb up! little boy,' said the Tree, and it bent its branches down as low as it could; but the boy was too tiny.

And the Giant's heart melted as he looked out. 'How selfish I have been!' he said; 'now I know why the Spring would not come here. I will put that poor little boy on the top of the tree, and then I will knock down the wall, and my garden shall be the children's playground for ever and ever.' He was really very sorry for what he had done.

So he crept downstairs and opened the front door quite softly, and went out into the garden. But when the children saw him they were so frightened that they all ran away, and the garden became winter again. Only the little boy did not run, for his eyes were so full of tears that he did not see the Giant coming. And the Giant stole up behind him and took him gently in his hand, and put him up into the tree. And the tree broke at once into blossom, and the birds came and sang on it, and the little boy stretched out his two arms and flung them round the Giant's neck, and kissed him. And the other children, when they saw that the Giant was not wicked any longer, came running back, and with them came the Spring. 'It is your garden now, little children,' said the Giant, and he took a great axe and knocked down the wall. And when the people were going to market at twelve o'clock they found the Giant playing with the children in the most beautiful garden they had ever seen.

All day long they played, and in the evening they came to the Giant to bid him good-bye.

'But where is your little companion?' he said: 'the boy I put into the tree.' The Giant loved him the best because he had kissed him.

'We don't know,' answered the children; 'he has gone away.'

'You must tell him to be sure and come here to-morrow,' said the Giant. But the children said that they did not know where he lived, and had never seen him before; and the Giant felt very sad.

Every afternoon, when school was over, the children came and played with the Giant. But the little boy whom the Giant loved was never seen again.

The Giant was very kind to all the children, yet he longed for his first little friend, and often spoke of him. 'How I would like to see him!' he used to say.

Years went over, and the Giant grew very old and feeble. He could not play about any more, so he sat in a huge armchair, and watched the children at their games, and admired his garden. 'I have many beautiful flowers,' he said; 'but the children are the most beautiful flowers of all.'

One winter morning he looked out of his window as he was dressing. He did not hate the Winter now, for he knew that it was merely the Spring asleep, and that the flowers were resting.

Suddenly he rubbed his eyes in wonder, and looked and looked. It certainly was a marvellous sight. In the farthest corner of the garden was a tree quite covered with lovely white blossoms. Its branches were all golden, and silver fruit hung down from them, and underneath it, stood the little boy he had loved.

Downstairs ran the Giant in great joy, and out into the garden. He hastened across the grass, and came near to the child. And when he came quite close, his face grew red with anger, and he said, 'Who hath dared to wound thee?' For on the palms of the child's hands were the prints of two nails, and the prints of two nails were on the little feet.

'Who hath dared to wound thee?' cried the Giant; 'tell me, that I may take my big sword and slay him.'

'Nay!' answered the child; 'but these are the wounds of Love.'

'Who art thou?' said the Giant, and a strange awe fell on him, and he knelt before the little child.

And the child smiled on the Giant, and said to him, 'You let me play once in your garden, to-day you shall come with me to my garden, which is Paradise.'

And when the children ran in that afternoon, they found the Giant lying dead under the tree, all covered with white blossoms.

CINDERELLA

Brothers Grimm

The wife of a rich man fell sick: and when she felt that her end drew nigh, she called her only daughter to her bedside, and said, 'Always be a good girl, and I will look down from heaven and watch over you.' Soon afterwards, she shut her eyes and died, and was buried in the garden; and the little girl went every day to her grave and wept, and was always good and kind to all about her. And the snow spread a beautiful white covering over the grave; but by the time the sun had melted it away again, her father had married another wife. This new wife had two daughters of her own: they were fair in face but foul at heart, and it was now a sorry time for the poor little girl. 'What does the good-for-nothing thing want in the parlour?' said they; and they took away her fine clothes, and gave her an old frock to put on, and laughed at her and turned her into the kitchen.

Then she was forced to do hard work; to rise early, before daylight, to bring the water, to make the fire, to cook and to wash. She had no bed to lie down on, but was made to lie by the hearth among the ashes, and they called her Cinderella.

It happened once that her father was going to the fair, and asked his wife's daughters what he should bring to them.

'Fine clothes,' said the first.

'Pearls and diamonds,' said the second.

'Now, child,' said he to his own daughter, 'what will you have?'

'The first sprig, dear father, that rubs against your hat on your way home,' said she. Then he bought for the two, first the fine clothes and pearls and diamonds they had asked for: and on his way home, as he rode through a green copse, a sprig of hazel brushed against him, so he broke it off and when he got home, he gave it to his daughter. Then she took it, and went to her mother's grave and planted it there, and cried so much that it was watered with her tears; and there it grew and became a fine tree, and soon a little bird came and built its nest upon the tree, and talked with her and watched over her, and brought her whatever she wished for.

Now it happened that the king of the land held a feast which was to last three days, and out of those who came to it his son was to choose a bride for himself; and Cinderella's two sisters were asked to come. So they called Cinderella, and said, 'Now, comb our hair, brush our shoes, and tie our sashes for us, for we are going to dance at the king's feast.' Then she did as she was told, but when all was done she could not help crying, for she thought to herself, she would have liked to go to the dance too, and at last she begged her mother very hard to let her go, 'You! Cinderella?' said she; 'You who have nothing to wear, no clothes at all, and who cannot even dance—you want to go to the ball?' And when she kept on begging, to get rid of her, she said at last, 'I will throw this basinful of peas into the ash heap, and if you have picked them all out in two hours' time, you shall go to the feast too.' Then she threw the peas into the ashes; but the little maiden ran out at the back door into the garden, and cried out—

'Hither, thither, through the sky, turtle-doves and linnets, fly!

Blackbird, thrush, and chaffinch gay, hither, thither, haste away!

One and all, come, help me quick! haste ye, haste ye—pick, pick, pick!'

Then first came two white doves; and next two turtle-doves; and after them all the little birds under heaven came, and the little doves stooped their heads down and set to work, pick, pick, pick; and then the others began to pick, pick, pick, and picked out all the good grain and put it into a dish, and left the ashes.

At the end of one hour, the work was done, and all flew out again at the windows. Then she brought the dish to her mother. But the mother said, 'No, no! Indeed, you have no clothes and cannot dance; you shall not go.' And when Cinderella begged very hard to go, she said, 'If you can in one hour's time pick two of these dishes of peas out of the ashes, you shall go too.' So she shook two more dishes of peas into the ashes; but the little maiden went out into the garden at the back of the house, and called as before and all the birds came flying, and in half an hour's time all was done, and out they flew again. And then Cinderella took the dishes to her mother, rejoicing to think that she should now go to the ball. But her mother said, 'It is all of no use, you cannot go; you have no clothes, and cannot dance; and you would only put us to shame;' and off she went with her two daughters to the feast.

Now when all were gone, and nobody left at home, Cinderella went sorrowfully and sat down under the hazel-tree, and cried out—

'Shake, shake, hazel-tree, gold and silver over me!'

Then her friend the bird flew out of the tree and brought a gold and silver dress for her, and slippers of spangled silk; and she put them on, and followed her sisters to the feast. But they did not know her, she looked so fine and beautiful in her rich clothes.

The king's son soon came up to her, and took her by the hand and danced with her and no one else; and he never left her hand, but when anyone else came to ask her to dance, he said, 'This lady is dancing with me.' Thus they danced till a late hour of the night, and then she wanted to go home; and the king's son said, 'I shall go and take care of you to your home,' for he wanted to see where the beautiful maid lived. But she slipped away from him unawares, and ran off towards home, and the prince followed her; then she jumped up into the pigeon-house and shut the door. So he waited till her father came home, and told him that the unknown maiden who had been at the feast had hidden herself in the pigeon-house. But when they had broken open the door they found no one within; and as they came back into the house, Cinderella lay, as she always did, in her dirty frock by the ashes; for she had run as quickly as she could through the pigeon-house and on to the hazel-tree, and had there taken off her beautiful clothes, and laid them beneath the tree, that the bird might carry them away; and had seated herself amid the ashes again in her little old frock.

The next day, when the feast was again held, and her father, mother and sisters were gone, Cinderella went to the hazel-tree, and all happened as the evening before.

The king's son, who was waiting for her, took her by the hand and danced with her; and, when any one asked her to dance, he said as before, 'This lady is dancing with me.' When night came she wanted to go home; and the king's son went with her, but she sprang away from him all at once into the garden behind her father's house. In this garden stood a fine large pear-tree; and Cinderella jumped up into it without being seen. Then the king's son waited till her father came home, and said to him, 'The unknown lady has slipped away, and I think she must have sprung into the pear-tree.' The father ordered an axe to be brought, and they cut down the tree, but found no one upon it. And when they came back into the kitchen, there lay Cinderella in the ashes as usual; for she had slipped down on the other side of the tree, and carried her beautiful clothes back to the bird at the hazel-tree, and then put on her little old frock.

The third day, when her father and mother and sisters were gone, she went again into the garden, and said—

'Shake, shake, hazel-tree, gold and silver over me!'

Then her kind friend the bird brought a dress still finer than the former one, and slippers which were all of gold; and the king's son danced with her alone, and when anyone else asked her to dance, he said, 'This lady is my partner.' Now when night came she wanted to go home; and the king's son would go with her, but she managed to slip away from him, though in such a hurry that she dropped her left golden slipper upon the stairs.

So the prince took the shoe, and went the next day to the king, his father, and said, 'I will take for my wife the lady that this golden shoe fits.'

Then both the sisters were overjoyed to hear this; for they had beautiful feet, and had no doubt that they could wear the golden slipper. The eldest went first into the room where the slipper was, and wanted to try it on, and the mother stood by. But her big toe could not go into it, and the shoe was altogether much too small for her. Then the mother said, 'Never mind, cut it off. When you are queen you will not care about toes; you will not want to go on foot.' So the silly girl cut her big toe off, and squeezed the shoe on, and went to the king's son. Then he took her for his bride, and rode away with her.

But on their way home, they had to pass by the hazel-tree that Cinderella had planted, and there sat a little dove on the branch, singing—

Back again! back again! look to the shoe!
The shoe is too small, and not made for you!
Prince! prince! look again for thy bride,
For she's not the true one that sits by thy side.

Then the prince looked at her foot, and saw by the blood that streamed from it what a trick she had played him. So he brought the false bride back to her home, and said, 'This is not the right bride; let the other sister try and put on the slipper.' Then she went into the room and got her foot into the shoe, all but the heel, which was too large. But her mother squeezed it in till the blood came, and took her to the king's son; and he rode away with her. But when they came to the hazel-tree, the little dove sat there still, and sang as before. Then the king's son looked down, and saw that the blood streamed from the shoe. So he brought her back again also. 'This is not the true bride,' said he to the father; 'have you no other daughters?'

Then Cinderella came and she took her clumsy shoe off, and put on the golden slipper, and it fitted as if it had been made for her. And when he drew near and looked at her face the prince knew her, and said, 'This is the right bride.'

Then he took Cinderella on his horse and rode away. And when they came to the hazel-tree the white dove sang—

'Prince! prince! take home thy bride,
For she is the true one that sits by thy side!'

THE LITTLE MERMAID

Hans Christian Andersen

Far out in the ocean, where the water is as blue as the prettiest cornflower, and as clear as crystal, it is very, very deep; so deep, indeed, that no cable could fathom it: many church steeples, piled one upon another, would not reach from the ground beneath to the surface of the water above. There dwell the Sea King and his subjects. We must not imagine that there is nothing at the bottom of the sea but bare yellow sand. No, indeed; the most singular flowers and plants grow there; the leaves and stems of which are so pliant, that the slightest agitation of the water causes them to stir as if they had life. Fishes, both large and small, glide between the branches, as birds fly among the trees here upon land. In the deepest spot of all, stands the castle of the Sea King. Its walls are built of coral, and the long, gothic windows are of the clearest amber. The roof is formed of shells, that open and close as the water flows over them. Their appearance is very beautiful, for in each lies a glittering pearl, which would be fit for the diadem of a queen.

The Sea King had been a widower for many years, and his aged mother kept house for him. She was a very wise woman, and exceedingly proud of her high birth; on that account she wore twelve oysters on her tail; while others, also of high rank, were only allowed to wear six. She was, however, deserving of very great praise, especially for her care of the little sea-princesses, her grand-daughters. They were six beautiful children; but the youngest was the prettiest of them all; her skin was as clear and delicate as a rose-leaf, and her eyes as blue as the deepest sea; but, like all the others, she had no feet, and her body ended in a fish's tail. All day long they played in the great halls of the castle, or among the living flowers that grew out of the walls. The large amber windows were open, and the fish swam in, just as the swallows fly into our houses when we open the windows, excepting that the fish swam up to the princesses, ate out of their hands, and allowed themselves to be stroked. Outside the castle, there was a beautiful garden, in which grew bright red and dark blue flowers, and blossoms like flames of fire; the fruit glittered like gold, and the leaves and stems waved to and fro continually. The earth itself was the finest sand, but blue as the flame of burning sulphur. Over everything lay a peculiar blue radiance, as if it were surrounded by the air from above, through which the blue sky shone, instead of the dark depths of the sea. In calm weather, the sun could be seen, looking like a purple flower, with the light streaming from the calyx. Each of the young princesses had a little plot of ground in the garden, where she might dig and plant as she pleased. One arranged her flower-bed into the form of a whale; another thought it better to make hers like the figure of a little mermaid; but that of the youngest was round like the sun, and contained flowers as red as his rays at sunset. She was a strange child, quiet and thoughtful; and while her sisters would be delighted with the wonderful things which they obtained from the wrecks of vessels, she cared for nothing but her pretty red flowers, like the sun, excepting a beautiful marble statue. It was the representation of a handsome boy, carved out of pure white stone, which had fallen to the bottom of the sea from a wreck. She planted by the statue a rose-coloured weeping willow. It grew splendidly, and very soon hung its fresh branches over the statue, almost down to the blue sands.

The shadow had a violet tint, and waved to and fro like the branches; it seemed as if the crown of the tree and the root were at play, and trying to kiss each other. Nothing gave her so much pleasure as to hear about the world above the sea. She made her old grandmother tell her all she knew of the ships and of the towns, the people and the animals. To her it seemed most wonderful and beautiful to hear that the flowers of the land should have fragrance, and not those below the sea; that the trees of the forest should be green; and that the fishes among the trees could sing so sweetly, that it was quite a pleasure to hear them. Her grandmother called the little birds fishes, or she would not have understood her; for she had never seen birds.

'When you have reached your fifteenth year,' said the grandmother, 'you will have permission to rise up out of the sea, to sit on the rocks in the moonlight, while the great ships are sailing by; and then you will see both forests and towns.'

In the following year, one of the sisters would be fifteen: but as each was a year younger than the other, the youngest would have to wait five years before her turn came to rise up from the bottom of the ocean, and see the earth as we do. However, each promised to tell the others what she saw on her first visit, and what she thought the most beautiful; for their grandmother could not tell them enough; there were so many things on which they wanted information. None of them longed so much for her turn to come as the youngest, she who had the longest time to wait, and who was so quiet and thoughtful. Many nights she stood by the open window, looking up through the dark blue water, and watching the fish as they splashed about with their fins and tails. She could see the moon and stars shining faintly; but through the water they looked larger than they do to our eyes. When something like a black cloud passed between her and them, she knew that it was either a whale swimming over her head, or a ship full of human beings, who never imagined that a pretty little mermaid was standing beneath them, holding out her white hands towards the keel of their ship.

As soon as the eldest was fifteen, she was allowed to rise to the surface of the ocean. When she came back, she had hundreds of things to talk about; but the most beautiful, she said, was to lie in the moonlight, on a sandbank, in the quiet sea, near the coast, and to gaze on a large town nearby, where the lights were twinkling like hundreds of stars; to listen to the sounds of the music, the noise of carriages, and the voices of human beings, and then to hear the merry bells peal out from the church steeples; and because she could not go near to all those wonderful things, she longed for them more than ever. Oh, did not the youngest sister listen eagerly to all these descriptions? and afterwards, when she stood at the open window looking up through the dark blue water, she thought of the great city, with all its bustle and noise, and even fancied she could hear the sound of the church bells, down in the depths of the sea.

In another year, the second sister received permission to rise to the surface of the water, and to swim about where she pleased. She rose just as the sun was setting, and this, she said, was the most beautiful sight of all. The whole sky looked like gold, while violet and rose-coloured clouds, which she could not describe, floated over her; and, still more rapidly than the clouds, flew a large flock of wild swans towards the setting sun, looking like a long white veil across the sea. She also swam towards the sun; but it sunk into the waves, and the rosy tints faded from the clouds and from the sea.

The third sister's turn followed; she was the boldest of them all, and she swam up a broad river that emptied itself into the sea. On the banks she saw green hills covered with beautiful vines; palaces and castles peeped out from amid the proud trees of the forest; she heard the birds singing, and the rays of the sun were so powerful that she was obliged often to dive down under the water to cool her burning face. In a narrow creek she found a whole troop of little human children, quite naked, and sporting about in the water; she wanted to play with them, but they fled in a great fright; and then a little black animal came to the water; it was a dog, but she did not know that, for she had never before seen one. This animal barked at her so terribly that she became frightened, and rushed back to the open sea. But she said she should never forget the beautiful forest, the green hills, and the pretty little children who could swim in the water, although they had not fish's tails.

The fourth sister was more timid; she remained in the midst of the sea, but she said it was quite as beautiful there as nearer the land. She could see for so many miles around her, and the sky above looked like a bell of glass. She had seen the ships, but at such a great distance that they looked like sea-gulls. The dolphins sported in the waves, and the great whales spouted water from their nostrils till it seemed as if a hundred fountains were playing in every direction.

The fifth sister's birthday occurred in the winter; so when her turn came, she saw what the others had not seen the first time they went up. The sea looked quite green, and large icebergs were floating about, each like a pearl, she said, but larger and loftier than the churches built by men. They were of the most singular shapes, and glittered like diamonds. She had seated herself upon one of the largest, and let the wind play with her long hair, and she remarked that all the ships sailed by rapidly, and steered as far away as they could from the iceberg, as if they were afraid of it. Towards evening, as the sun went down, dark clouds covered the sky, the thunder rolled and the lightning flashed, and the red light glowed on the icebergs as they rocked and tossed on the heaving sea. On all the ships the sails were reefed with fear and trembling, while she sat calmly on the floating iceberg, watching the blue lightning, as it darted its forked flashes into the sea.

When first the sisters had permission to rise to the surface, they were each delighted with the new and beautiful sights they saw; but now, as grown-up girls, they could go when they pleased, and they had become indifferent about it. They wished themselves back again in the water, and after a month had passed they said it was much more beautiful down below, and pleasanter to be at home. Yet often, in the evening hours, the five sisters would twine their arms round each other, and rise to the surface, in a row. They had more beautiful voices than any human being could have; and before the approach of a storm, and when they expected a ship would be lost, they swam before the vessel, and sang sweetly of the delights to be found in the depths of the sea, and begging the sailors not to fear if they sank to the bottom. But the sailors could not understand the song, they took it for the howling of the storm. And these things were never to be beautiful for them; for if the ship sank, the men were drowned, and their dead bodies alone reached the palace of the Sea King.

When the sisters rose, arm-in-arm, through the water in this way, their youngest sister would stand quite alone, looking after them, ready to cry, only that the mermaids have no tears, and therefore they suffer more. 'Oh, were I but fifteen years old,' said she: 'I know that I shall love the world up there, and all the people who live in it.'

At last she reached her fifteenth year. 'Well, now, you are grown up,' said the old dowager, her grandmother; 'so you must let me adorn you like your other sisters;' and she placed a wreath of white lilies in her hair, and every flower leaf was half a pearl. Then the old lady ordered eight great oysters to attach themselves to the tail of the princess to show her high rank.

'But they hurt me so,' said the little mermaid.

'Pride must suffer pain,' replied the old lady. Oh, how gladly she would have shaken off all this grandeur, and laid aside the heavy wreath! The red flowers in her own garden would have suited her much better, but she could not help herself: so she said, 'Farewell,' and rose as lightly as a bubble to the surface of the water. The sun had just set as she raised her head above the waves; but the clouds were tinted with crimson and gold, and through the glimmering twilight beamed the evening star in all its beauty. The sea was calm, and the air mild and fresh. A large ship, with three masts, lay becalmed on the water, with only one sail set; for not a breeze stiffed, and the sailors sat idle on deck or amongst the rigging. There was music and song on board; and, as darkness came on, a hundred coloured lanterns were lighted, as if the flags of all nations waved in the air. The little mermaid swam close to the cabin windows; and now and then, as the waves lifted her up, she could look in through clear glass window-panes, and see a number of well-dressed people within. Among them was a young prince, the most beautiful of all, with large black eyes; he was sixteen years of age, and his birthday was being kept with much rejoicing. The sailors were dancing on deck, but when the prince came out of the cabin, more than a hundred rockets rose in the air, making it as bright as day. The little mermaid was so startled that she dived under water; and when she again stretched out her head, it appeared as if all the stars of heaven were falling around her, she had never seen such fireworks before. Great suns spurted fire about, splendid fireflies flew into the blue air, and everything was reflected in the clear, calm sea beneath. The ship itself was so brightly illuminated that all the people, and even the smallest rope, could be distinctly and plainly seen. And how handsome the young prince looked, as he pressed the hands of all present and smiled at them, while the music resounded through the clear night air.

It was very late; yet the little mermaid could not take her eyes from the ship, or from the beautiful prince. The coloured lanterns had been extinguished, no more rockets rose in the air, and the cannon had ceased firing; but the sea became restless, and a moaning, grumbling sound could be heard beneath the waves: still the little mermaid remained by the cabin window, rocking up and down on the water, which enabled her to look in. After a while, the sails were quickly unfurled, and the noble ship continued her passage; but soon the waves rose higher, heavy clouds darkened the sky, and lightning appeared in the distance. A dreadful storm was approaching; once more the sails were reefed, and the great ship pursued her flying course over the raging sea. The waves rose mountains high, as if they would have overtopped the mast; but the ship dived like a swan between them, and then rose again on their lofty, foaming crests. To the little mermaid, this appeared pleasant sport; not so to the sailors.

At length the ship groaned and creaked; the thick planks gave way under the lashing of the sea as it broke over the deck; the mainmast snapped asunder like a reed; the ship lay over on her side; and the water rushed in. The little mermaid now perceived that the crew were in danger; even she herself was obliged to be careful to avoid the beams and planks of the wreck which lay scattered on the water. At one moment it was so pitch dark that she could not see a single object, but a flash of lightning revealed the whole scene; she could see everyone who had been on board excepting the prince; when the ship parted, she had seen him sink into the deep waves, and she was glad, for she thought he would now be with her;

and then she remembered that human beings could not live in the water, so that when he got down to her father's palace he would be quite dead. But he must not die. So she swam about among the beams and planks which strewed the surface of the sea, forgetting that they could crush her to pieces. Then she dived deeply under the dark waters, rising and falling with the waves, till at length she managed to reach the young prince, who was fast losing the power of swimming in that stormy sea. His limbs were failing him, his beautiful eyes were closed, and he would have died had not the little mermaid come to his assistance. She held his head above the water, and let the waves drift them where they would.

In the morning, the storm had ceased; but of the ship not a single fragment could be seen. The sun rose up red and glowing from the water, and its beams brought back the hue of health to the prince's cheeks; but his eyes remained closed. The mermaid kissed his high, smooth forehead, and stroked back his wet hair; he seemed to her like the marble statue in her little garden, and she kissed him again, and wished that he might live. Presently they came in sight of land; she saw lofty blue mountains, on which the white snow rested as if a flock of swans were lying upon them. Near the coast were beautiful green forests, and close by stood a large building, whether a church or a convent she could not tell. Orange and citron trees grew in the garden, and before the door stood lofty palms. The sea here formed a little bay, in which the water was quite still, but very deep; so she swam with the handsome prince to the beach, which was covered with fine, white sand, and there she laid him in the warm sunshine, taking care to raise his head higher than his body. Then bells sounded in the large white building, and a number of young girls came into the garden. The little mermaid swam out farther from the shore and placed herself between some high rocks that rose out of the water; then she covered her head and neck with the foam of the sea so that her little face might not be seen, and watched to see what would become of the poor prince.

She did not wait long before she saw a young girl approach the spot where he lay. She seemed frightened at first, but only for a moment; then she fetched a number of people, and the mermaid saw that the prince came to life again, and smiled upon those who stood round him. But to her he sent no smile; he knew not that she had saved him. This made her very unhappy, and when he was led away into the great building, she dived down sorrowfully into the water, and returned to her father's castle. She had always been silent and thoughtful, and now she was more so than ever.

Her sisters asked her what she had seen during her first visit to the surface of the water; but she would tell them nothing. Many an evening and morning did she rise to the place where she had left the prince. She saw the fruits in the garden ripen till they were gathered, the snow on the tops of the mountains melt away; but she never saw the prince, and therefore she returned home, always more sorrowful than before. It was her only comfort to sit in her own little garden, and fling her arm around the beautiful marble statue which was like the prince; but she gave up tending her flowers, and they grew in wild confusion over the paths, twining their long leaves and stems round the branches of the trees, so that the whole place became dark and gloomy.

At length she could bear it no longer, and told one of her sisters all about it. Then the others heard the secret, and very soon it became known to two mermaids whose intimate friend happened to know who the prince was. She had also seen the festival on board ship, and she told them where the prince came from, and where his palace stood.

'Come, little sister,' said the other princesses; then they entwined their arms and rose up in a long row to the surface of the water, close by the spot where they knew the prince's palace stood. It was built of bright yellow shining stone, with long flights of marble steps, one of which reached quite down to the sea. Splendid gilded cupolas rose over the roof, and between the pillars that surrounded the whole building stood life-like statues of marble. Through the clear crystal of the lofty windows could be seen noble rooms, with costly silk curtains and hangings of tapestry; while the walls were covered with beautiful paintings which were a pleasure to look at. In the centre of the largest saloon, a fountain threw its sparkling jets high up into the glass cupola of the ceiling, through which the sun shone down upon the water and upon the beautiful plants growing round the basin of the fountain.

Now that she knew where he lived, she spent many an evening and many a night on the water near the palace. She would swim much nearer the shore than any of the others ventured to do; indeed once she went quite up the narrow channel under the marble balcony, which threw a broad shadow on the water. Here she would sit and watch the young prince, who thought himself quite alone in the bright moonlight. She saw him many times of an evening sailing in a pleasant boat, with music playing and flags waving. She peeped out from among the green rushes, and if the wind caught her long silvery-white veil, those who saw it believed it to be a swan, spreading out its wings. On many a night, too, when the fishermen, with their torches, were out at sea, she heard them relate so many good things about the doings of the young prince, that she was glad she had saved his life when he had been tossed about half-dead on the waves. And she remembered that his head had rested on her bosom, and how heartily she had kissed him; but he knew nothing of all this, and could not even dream of her. She grew more and more fond of human beings, and wished more and more to be able to wander about with those whose world seemed to be so much larger than her own.

They could fly over the sea in ships, and mount the high hills which were far above the clouds; and the lands they possessed, their woods and their fields, stretched far away beyond the reach of her sight. There was so much that she wished to know, and her sisters were unable to answer all her questions. Then she applied to her old grandmother, who knew all about the upper world, which she very rightly called the lands above the sea.

'If human beings are not drowned,' asked the little mermaid, 'can they live forever? Do they never die as we do here in the sea?'

'Yes,' replied the old lady, 'they must also die, and their term of life is even shorter than ours. We sometimes live to three hundred years, but when we cease to exist here we only become the foam on the surface of the water, and we have not even a grave down here of those we love. We have not immortal souls, we shall never live again; but, like the green sea-weed, when once it has been cut off, we can never flourish more. Human beings, on the contrary, have a soul which lives forever, lives after the body has been turned to dust. It rises up through the clear, pure air beyond the glittering stars. As we rise out of the water, and behold all the land of the earth, so do they rise to unknown and glorious regions which we shall never see.'

'Why have not we an immortal soul?' asked the little mermaid mournfully; 'I would give gladly all the hundreds of years that I have to live, to be a human being only for one day, and to have the hope of knowing the happiness of that glorious world above the stars.'

'You must not think of that,' said the old woman; 'we feel ourselves to be much happier and much better off than human beings.'

'So I shall die,' said the little mermaid, 'and as the foam of the sea I shall be driven about never again to hear the music of the waves, or to see the pretty flowers nor the red sun. Is there anything I can do to win an immortal soul?'

'No,' said the old woman, 'unless a man were to love you so much that you were more to him than his father or mother; and if all his thoughts and all his love were fixed upon you, and the priest placed his right hand in yours, and he promised to be true to you here and hereafter, then his soul would glide into your body and you would obtain a share in the future happiness of mankind. He would give a soul to you and retain his own as well; but this can never happen. Your fish's tail, which amongst us is considered so beautiful, is thought on earth to be quite ugly; they do not know any better, and they think it necessary to have two stout props, which they call legs, in order to be handsome.'

Then the little mermaid sighed, and looked sorrowfully at her fish's tail. 'Let us be happy,' said the old lady, 'and dart and spring about during the three hundred years that we have to live, which is really quite long enough; after that we can rest ourselves all the better. This evening we are going to have a court ball.'

It is one of those splendid sights which we can never see on earth. The walls and the ceiling of the large ball-room were of thick, but transparent crystal. Hundreds of colossal shells, some of a deep red, others of a grass green, stood on each side in rows, with blue fire in them, which lighted up the whole saloon, and shone through the walls, so that the sea was also illuminated. Innumerable fishes, great and small, swam past the crystal walls; on some of them the scales glowed with a purple brilliancy, and on others, they shone like silver and gold. Through the halls flowed a broad stream, and in it danced the mermen and the mermaids to the music of their own sweet singing. No one on earth has such a lovely voice as theirs. The little mermaid sang more sweetly than them all. The whole court applauded her with hands and tails; and for a moment her heart felt quite gay, for she knew she had the loveliest voice of any on earth or in the sea.

But she soon thought again of the world above her, for she could not forget the charming prince, nor her sorrow that she had not an immortal soul like his; therefore, she crept away silently out of her father's palace, and while everything within was gladness and song, she sat in her own little garden, sorrowful and alone. Then she heard the bugle sounding through the water, and thought—'He is certainly sailing above, he on whom my wishes depend, and in whose hands I should like to place the happiness of my life. I will venture all for him, and to win an immortal soul, while my sisters are dancing in my father's palace, I will go to the sea witch, of whom I have always been so much afraid, but she can give me counsel and help.'

And then the little mermaid went out from her garden, and took the road to the foaming whirlpools, behind which the sorceress lived. She had never been that way before: neither flowers nor grass grew there; nothing but bare, grey, sandy ground stretched out to the whirlpool, where the water, like foaming mill-wheels, whirled round everything that it seized, and cast it into the fathomless deep. Through the midst of these crushing whirlpools, the little mermaid was obliged to pass, to reach the dominions of the sea witch; and also for a long distance the only road lay right across a quantity of warm, bubbling mire, called by the witch, her turf moor. Beyond this stood her house, in the centre of a strange forest, in which all the trees and flowers were polypi, half animals and half plants; they looked like serpents with a hundred heads growing out of the ground. The branches were long slimy arms, with fingers like flexible worms, moving limb after limb from the root to the top. All that could be reached in the sea they seized upon, and held fast, so that it never escaped from their clutches.

The little mermaid was so alarmed at what she saw, that she stood still, and her heart beat with fear, and she was very nearly turning back; but she thought of the prince, and of the human soul for which she longed, and her courage returned. She fastened her long flowing hair round her head, so that the polypi might not seize hold of it. She laid her hands together across her bosom, and then she darted forward as a fish shoots through the water, between the supple arms and fingers of the ugly polypi, which were stretched out on each side of her. She saw that each held in its grasp something it had seized with its numerous little arms, as if they were iron bands. The white skeletons of human beings who had perished at sea, and had sunk down into the deep waters, skeletons of land animals, oars, rudders, and chests of ships were lying tightly grasped by their clinging arms; even a little mermaid, whom they had caught and strangled; and this seemed the most shocking of all to the little princess.

She now came to a space of marshy ground in the wood, where large, fat water-snakes were rolling in the mire, and showing their ugly, drab-coloured bodies. In the midst of this spot stood a house, built with the bones of shipwrecked human beings. There sat the sea witch, allowing a toad to eat from her mouth, just as people sometimes feed a canary with a piece of sugar. She called the ugly water-snakes her little chickens, and allowed them to crawl all over her bosom.

'I know what you want,' said the sea witch; 'it is very stupid of you, but you shall have your way, and it will bring you to sorrow, my pretty princess. You want to get rid of your fish's tail, and to have two supports instead of it, like human beings on earth, so that the young prince may fall in love with you, and that you may have an immortal soul.' And then the witch laughed so loud and disgustingly, that the toad and the snakes fell to the ground, and lay there wriggling about. 'You are but just in time,' said the witch; 'for after sunrise to-morrow I should not be able to help you till the end of another year. I will prepare a draught for you, with which you must swim to land tomorrow before sunrise, and sit down on the shore and drink it. Your tail will then disappear, and shrink up into what mankind calls legs, and you will feel great pain, as if a sword were passing through you. But all who see you will say that you are the prettiest little human being they ever saw. You will still have the same floating gracefulness of movement, and no dancer will ever tread so lightly; but at every step you take, it will feel as if you were treading upon sharp knives, and that the blood must flow. If you will bear all this, I will help you.'

'Yes, I will,' said the little princess in a trembling voice, as she thought of the prince and the immortal soul.

'But think again,' said the witch; 'for when once your shape has become like a human being, you can no more be a mermaid. You will never return through the water to your sisters, or to your father's palace again; and if you do not win the love of the prince, so that he is willing to forget his father and mother for your sake, and to love you with his whole soul, and allow the priest to join your hands that you may be man and wife, then you will never have an immortal soul. The first morning after he marries another your heart will break, and you will become foam on the crest of the waves.'

'I will do it,' said the little mermaid, and she became pale as death.

'But I must be paid also,' said the witch, 'and it is not a trifle that I ask. You have the sweetest voice of any who dwell here in the depths of the sea, and you believe that you will be able to charm the prince with it also, but this voice you must give to me; the best thing you possess will I have for the price of my draught. My own blood must be mixed with it, that it may be as sharp as a two-edged sword.'

'But if you take away my voice,' said the little mermaid, 'what is left for me?'

'Your beautiful form, your graceful walk, and your expressive eyes; surely with these you can enchain a man's heart. Well, have you lost your courage? Put out your little tongue that I may cut it off as my payment; then you shall have the powerful draught.'

'It shall be,' said the little mermaid.

Then the witch placed her cauldron on the fire, to prepare the magic draught.

'Cleanliness is a good thing,' said she, scouring the vessel with snakes, which she had tied together in a large knot; then she pricked herself in the breast, and let the black blood drop into it. The steam that rose formed itself into such horrible shapes that no one could look at them without fear. Every moment the witch threw something else into the vessel, and when it began to boil, the sound was like the weeping of a crocodile. When at last the magic draught was ready, it looked like the clearest water. 'There it is for you,' said the witch. Then she cut off the mermaid's tongue, so that she became dumb, and would never again speak or sing. 'If the polypi should seize hold of you as you return through the wood,' said the witch, 'throw over them a few drops of the potion, and their fingers will be torn into a thousand pieces.' But the little mermaid had no occasion to do this, for the polypi sprang back in terror when they caught sight of the glittering draught, which shone in her hand like a twinkling star.

So she passed quickly through the wood and the

marsh, and between the rushing whirlpools. She saw that in her father's palace the torches in the ballroom were extinguished, and all within asleep; but she did not venture to go in to them, for now she was dumb and going to leave them forever, she felt as if her heart would break. She stole into the garden, took a flower from the flower-beds of each of her sisters, kissed her hand a thousand times towards the palace, and then rose up through the dark blue waters. The sun had not risen when she came in sight of the prince's palace, and approached the beautiful marble steps, but the moon shone clear and bright. Then the little mermaid drank the magic draught, and it seemed as if a two-edged sword went through her delicate body: she fell into a swoon, and lay like one dead. When the sun arose and shone over the sea, she recovered, and felt a sharp pain; but just before her stood the handsome young prince. He fixed his coal-black eyes upon her so earnestly that she cast down her own, and then became aware that her fish's tail was gone, and that she had as pretty a pair of white legs and tiny feet as any little maiden could have; but she had no clothes, so she wrapped herself in her long, thick hair.

The prince asked her who she was, and where she came from, and she looked at him mildly and sorrowfully with her deep blue eyes; but she could not speak. Every step she took was as the witch had said it would be, she felt as if treading upon the points of needles or sharp knives; but she bore it willingly, and stepped as lightly by the prince's side as a soap-bubble, so that he and all who saw her wondered at her graceful-swaying movements. She was very soon arrayed in costly robes of silk and muslin, and was the most beautiful creature in the palace; but she was dumb, and could neither speak nor sing.

Beautiful female slaves, dressed in silk and gold, stepped forward and sang before the prince and his royal parents: one sang better than all the others, and the prince clapped his hands and smiled at her. This was great sorrow to the little mermaid; she knew how much more sweetly she herself could sing once, and she thought, 'Oh if he could only know that! I have given away my voice forever, to be with him.'

The slaves next performed some pretty fairy-like dances, to the sound of beautiful music. Then the little mermaid raised her lovely white arms, stood on the tips of her toes, and glided over the floor, and danced as no one yet had been able to dance. At each moment her beauty became more revealed, and her expressive eyes appealed more directly to the heart than the songs of the slaves. Everyone was enchanted, especially the prince, who called her his little foundling; and she danced again quite readily, to please him, though each time her foot touched the floor, it seemed as if she trod on sharp knives.

The prince said she should remain with him always, and she received permission to sleep at his door, on a velvet cushion. He had a page's dress made for her, that she might accompany him on horseback. They rode together through the sweet-scented woods, where the green boughs touched their shoulders, and the little birds sang among the fresh leaves. She climbed with the prince to the tops of high mountains; and although her tender feet bled so that even her steps were marked, she only laughed, and followed him till they could see the clouds beneath them looking like a flock of birds travelling to distant lands. While at the prince's palace, and when all the household were asleep, she would go and sit on the broad marble steps; for it eased her burning feet to bathe them in the cold sea-water; and then she thought of all those below in the deep.

Once during the night, her sisters came up arm-in-arm, singing sorrowfully, as they floated on the water. She beckoned to them, and then they recognised her, and told her how she had grieved them. After that, they came to the same place every night; and once she saw in the distance, her old grandmother, who had not been to the surface of the sea for many years, and the old Sea King, her father, with his crown on his head. They stretched out their hands towards her, but they did not venture so near the land as her sisters did.

As the days passed, she loved the prince more fondly, and he loved her as he would love a little child, but it never came into his head to make her his wife; yet, unless he married her, she could not receive an immortal soul and, on the morning after his marriage with another, she would dissolve into the foam of the sea.

'Do you not love me the best of them all?' the eyes of the little mermaid seemed to say, when he took her in his arms, and kissed her fair forehead.

'Yes, you are dear to me,' said the prince; 'for you have the best heart, and you are the most devoted to me; you are like a young maiden whom I once saw, but whom I shall never meet again. I was in a ship that was wrecked, and the waves cast me ashore near a holy temple, where several young maidens performed the service. The youngest of them found me on the shore, and saved my life. I saw her but twice, and she is the only one in the world whom I could love; but you are like her, and you have almost driven her image out of my mind. She belongs to the holy temple, and my good fortune has sent you to me instead of her; and we will never part.'

'Ah, he knows not that it was I who saved his life,' thought the little mermaid. 'I carried him over the sea to the wood where the temple stands: I sat beneath the foam, and watched till the human beings came to help him. I saw the pretty maiden that he loves better than he loves me;' and the mermaid sighed deeply, but she could not shed tears. 'He says the maiden belongs to the holy temple, therefore, she will never return to the world. They will meet no more: while I am by his side, and see him every day. I will take care of him, and love him, and give up my life for his sake.'

Very soon it was said that the prince must marry, and that the beautiful daughter of a neighbouring king would be his wife, for a fine ship was being fitted out. Although the prince gave out that he merely intended to pay a visit to the king, it was generally supposed that he really went to see his daughter. A great company were to go with him. The little mermaid smiled, and shook her head. She knew the prince's thoughts better than any of the others.

'I must travel,' he had said to her; 'I must see this beautiful princess; my parents' desire it; but they will not oblige me to bring her home as my bride. I cannot love her; she is not like the beautiful maiden in the temple, whom you resemble. If I were forced to choose a bride, I would rather choose you, my dumb foundling, with those expressive eyes.' And then he kissed her rosy mouth, played with her long waving hair, and laid his head on her heart, while she dreamed of human happiness and an immortal soul. 'You are not afraid of the sea, my dumb child,' said he, as they stood on the deck of the noble ship which was to carry them to the country of the neighbouring king. And then he told her of storm and of calm, of strange fish in the deep beneath them, and of what the divers had seen there; and she smiled at his descriptions, for she knew better than anyone what wonders were at the bottom of the sea.

In the moonlight, when all on board were asleep, excepting the man at the helm, who was steering, she sat on the deck, gazing down through the clear water. She thought she could distinguish her father's castle, and upon it her aged grandmother, with the silver crown on her head, looking through the rushing tide at the keel of the vessel. Then her sisters came up on the waves, and gazed at her mournfully, wringing their white hands. She beckoned to them, and smiled, and wanted to tell them how happy and well off she was; but the cabin-boy approached, and when her sisters dived down, he thought it was only the foam of the sea which he saw.

The next morning, the ship sailed into the harbour of a beautiful town belonging to the king whom the prince was going to visit. The church bells were ringing, and from the high towers sounded a flourish of trumpets; and soldiers, with flying colours and glittering bayonets, lined the rocks through which they passed. Every day was a festival; balls and entertainments followed one another.

But the princess had not yet appeared. People said that she was being brought up and educated in a religious house, where she was learning every royal virtue. At last she came. Then the little mermaid, who was very anxious to see whether she was really beautiful, was obliged to acknowledge that she had never seen a more perfect vision of beauty. Her skin was delicately fair, and beneath her long dark eye-lashes, her laughing blue eyes shone with truth and purity.

'It was you,' said the prince, 'who saved my life when I lay dead on the beach,' and he folded his blushing bride in his arms. 'Oh, I am too happy,' said he to the little mermaid; 'my fondest hopes are all fulfilled. You will rejoice at my happiness; for your devotion to me is great and sincere.'

The little mermaid kissed his hand, and felt as if her heart were already broken. His wedding morning would bring death to her, and she would change into the foam of the sea. All the church bells rung, and the heralds rode about the town proclaiming the betrothal.

Perfumed oil was burning in costly silver lamps on every altar. The priests waved the censers, while the bride and bridegroom joined their hands and received the blessing of the bishop. The little mermaid, dressed in silk and gold, held up the bride's train; but her ears heard nothing of the festive music, and her eyes saw not the holy ceremony; she thought of the night of death which was coming to her, and of all she had lost in the world. On the same evening, the bride and bridegroom went on board ship; cannons were roaring, flags waving, and in the centre of the ship a costly tent of purple and gold had been erected. It contained elegant couches, for the reception of the bridal pair during the night. The ship, with swelling sails and a favourable wind, glided away smoothly and lightly over the calm sea. When it grew dark, a number of coloured lamps were lit, and the sailors danced merrily on the deck. The little mermaid could not help thinking of her first rising out of the sea, when she had seen similar festivities and joys; and she joined in the dance, poised herself in the air as a swallow when he pursues his prey, and all present cheered her with wonder. She had never danced so elegantly before. Her tender feet felt as if cut with sharp knives, but she cared not for it; a sharper pang had pierced through her heart. She knew this was the last evening she should ever see the prince, for whom she had forsaken her kindred and her home; she had given up her beautiful voice, and suffered unheard-of pain daily for him, while he knew nothing of it. This was the last evening that she would breathe the same air with him, or gaze on the starry sky and the deep sea; an eternal night, without a thought or a dream, awaited her: she had no soul and now she could never win one. All was joy and gaiety on board ship till long after midnight; she laughed and danced with the rest, while the thoughts of death were in her heart. The prince kissed his beautiful bride, while she played with his raven hair, till they went arm-in-arm to rest in the splendid tent. Then all became still on board the ship; the helmsman, alone awake, stood at the helm. The little mermaid leaned her white arms on the edge of the vessel, and looked towards the east for the first blush of morning, for that first ray of dawn that would bring her death. She saw her sisters rising out of the flood: they were as pale as herself; but their long beautiful hair waved no more in the wind, and had been cut off.

'We have given our hair to the witch,' said they, 'to obtain help for you, that you may not die tonight. She has given us a knife: here it is, see it is very sharp. Before the sun rises, you must plunge it into the heart of the prince; when the warm blood falls upon your feet they will grow together again, and form into a fish's tail, and you will be once more a mermaid, and return to us to live out your three hundred years before you die and change into the salt sea foam. Haste, then; he or you must die before sunrise. Our old grandmother moans so for you, that her white hair is falling off from sorrow, as ours fell under the witch's scissors. Kill the prince and come back; hasten: do you not see the first red streaks in the sky? In a few minutes, the sun will rise, and you must die.' And then they sighed deeply and mournfully, and sank down beneath the waves.

The little mermaid drew back the crimson curtain of the tent, and beheld the fair bride with her head resting on the prince's breast. She bent down and kissed his fair brow, then looked at the sky on which the rosy dawn grew brighter and brighter; then she glanced at the sharp knife, and again fixed her eyes on the prince, who whispered the name of his bride in his dreams. She was in his thoughts, and the knife trembled in the hand of the little mermaid: then she flung it far away from her into the waves; the water turned red where it fell, and the drops that spurted up looked like blood. She cast one more lingering, half-fainting glance at the prince, and then threw herself from the ship into the sea, and thought her body was dissolving into foam. The sun rose above the waves, and his warm rays fell on the cold foam of the little mermaid, who did not feel as if she were dying. She saw the bright sun, and all around her floated hundreds of transparent beautiful beings; she could see through them the white sails of the ship, and the red clouds in the sky; their speech was melodious, but too ethereal to be heard by mortal ears, as they were also unseen by mortal eyes.

The little mermaid perceived that she had a body like theirs, and that she continued to rise higher and higher out of the foam. 'Where am I?' asked she, and her voice sounded ethereal, as the voice of those who were with her; no earthly music could imitate it.

'Among the daughters of the air,' answered one of

them. 'A mermaid has not an immortal soul, nor can she obtain one unless she wins the love of a human being. On the power of another hangs her eternal destiny. But the daughters of the air, although they do not possess an immortal soul, can, by their good deeds, procure one for themselves. We fly to warm countries, and cool the sultry air that destroys mankind with the pestilence. We carry the perfume of the flowers to spread health and restoration. After we have striven for three hundred years to all the good in our power, we receive an immortal soul and take part in the happiness of mankind. You, poor little mermaid, have tried with your whole heart to do as we are doing; you have suffered and endured and raised yourself to the spirit-world by your good deeds; and now, by striving for three hundred years in the same way, you may obtain an immortal soul.'

The little mermaid lifted her glorified eyes towards the sun, and felt them, for the first time, filling with tears. On the ship, in which she had left the prince, there were life and noise; she saw him and his beautiful bride searching for her; sorrowfully they gazed at the pearly foam, as if they knew she had thrown herself into the waves. Unseen she kissed the forehead of the bride, and fanned the prince, and then mounted with the other children of the air to a rosy cloud that floated through the ether.

'After three hundred years, thus shall we float into the kingdom of heaven,' said she. 'And we may even get there sooner,' whispered one of her companions. 'Unseen, we can enter the houses of men, where there are children, and for every day on which we find a good child, who is the joy of his parents and deserves their love, our time of probation is shortened. The child does not know, when we fly through the room, that we smile with joy at his good conduct, for we can count one year less of our three hundred years. But when we see a naughty or a wicked child, we shed tears of sorrow, and for every tear a day is added to our time of trial!'

HANSEL AND GRETEL

Brothers Grimm

Hard by a great forest dwelt a poor wood-cutter with his wife and his two children. The boy was called Hansel and the girl, Gretel. He had little to bite and to break, and once when great dearth fell on the land, he could no longer procure even daily bread. Now when he thought over this by night in his bed, and tossed about in his anxiety, he groaned and said to his wife: 'What is to become of us? How are we to feed our poor children, when we no longer have anything even for ourselves?'

'I'll tell you what, husband,' answered the woman, 'early tomorrow morning, we will take the children out into the forest to where it is the thickest; there we will light a fire for them, and give each of them, one more piece of bread, and then we will go to our work and leave them alone. They will not find the way home again, and we shall be rid of them.'

'No, wife,' said the man, 'I will not do that; how can I bear to leave my children alone in the forest?—the wild animals would soon come and tear them to pieces.'

'O, you fool!' said she, 'then we must all four die of hunger, you may as well plane the planks for our coffins,' and she left him no peace until he consented.

'But I feel very sorry for the poor children, all the same,' said the man.

The two children had also not been able to sleep for hunger, and had heard what their stepmother had said to their father. Gretel wept bitter tears, and said to Hansel: 'Now all is over with us.'

'Be quiet, Gretel,' said Hansel, 'do not distress yourself, I will soon find a way to help us.' And when the old folks had fallen asleep, he got up, put on his little coat, opened the door below, and crept outside. The moon shone brightly, and the white pebbles which lay in front of the house glittered like real silver pennies. Hansel stooped and stuffed the little pocket of his coat with as many as he could get in. Then he went back and said to Gretel: 'Be comforted, dear little sister, and sleep in peace, God will not forsake us,' and he lay down again in his bed.

When day dawned, but before the sun had risen, the woman came and awoke the two children, saying: 'Get up, you sluggards! we are going into the forest to fetch wood.' She gave each a little piece of bread, and said: 'There is something for your dinner, but do not eat it up before then, for you will get nothing else.' Gretel took the bread under her apron, as Hansel had the pebbles in his pocket. Then, they all set out together on the way to the forest. When they had walked a short time, Hansel stood still and peeped back at the house, and did so again and again.

His father said: 'Hansel, what are you looking at there and staying behind for? Pay attention, and do not forget how to use your legs.'

'Ah, father,' said Hansel, 'I am looking at my little white cat, which is sitting up on the roof, and wants to say goodbye to me.'

The wife said: 'Fool, that is not your little cat, that is the morning sun which is shining on the chimneys.'

Hansel, however, had not been looking back at the cat, but had been constantly throwing one of the white pebble-stones out of his pocket on the road.

When they had reached the middle of the forest, the father said: 'Now, children, pile up some wood, and I will light a fire that you may not be cold.' Hansel and Gretel gathered brushwood together, as high as a little hill.

The brushwood was lighted, and when the flames were burning very high, the woman said: 'Now, children, lay yourselves down by the fire and rest, we will go into the forest and cut some wood. When we have done, we will come back and fetch you away.'

Hansel and Gretel sat by the fire, and when noon came, each ate a little piece of bread, and as they heard the strokes of the wood-axe they believed that their father was near. It was not the axe, however, but a branch which he had fastened to a withered tree which the wind was blowing backwards and forwards. And as they had been sitting such a long time, their eyes closed with fatigue, they fell fast asleep. When at last they awoke, it was already dark night. Gretel began to cry and said: 'How are we to get out of the forest now?' But Hansel comforted her and said: 'Just wait a little, until the moon has risen, and then we will soon find the way.' And when the full moon had risen, Hansel took his little sister by the hand, and followed the pebbles which shone like newly-coined silver pieces, and showed them the way.

They walked the whole night long, and by break of day came once more to their father's house. They knocked at the door, and when the woman opened it and saw that it was Hansel and Gretel, she said: 'You naughty children, why have you slept so long in the forest?—we thought you were never coming back at all!' The father, however, rejoiced, for it had cut him to the heart to leave them behind alone.

Not long afterwards, there was once more a great dearth throughout the land, and the children heard their mother saying at night to their father: 'Everything is eaten again, we have one half loaf left, and that is the end. The children must go, we will take them farther into the wood, so that they will not find their way out again; there is no other means of saving ourselves!'

The man's heart was heavy, and he thought: 'It would be better for you to share the last mouthful with your children.' The woman, however, would listen to nothing that he had to say, but scolded and reproached him. He who says A must say B, likewise, and as he had yielded the first time, he had to do so a second time, also.

The children, however, were still awake and had heard the conversation. When the old folks were asleep, Hansel again got up, and wanted to go out and pick up pebbles as he had done before, but the woman had locked the door, and Hansel could not get out. Nevertheless he comforted his little sister, and said: 'Do not cry, Gretel, go to sleep quietly; the good God will help us.'

Early in the morning came the woman, and took the children out of their beds. Their piece of bread was given to them, but it was still smaller than the time before. On the way into the forest, Hansel crumbled his in his pocket, and often stood still and threw a morsel on the ground.

'Hansel, why do you stop and look round?' said the father, 'go on.'

'I am looking back at my little pigeon which is sitting on the roof, and wants to say goodbye to me,' answered Hansel.

'Fool!' said the woman, 'that is not your little pigeon, that is the morning sun that is shining on the chimney.'

Hansel, however little by little, threw all the crumbs on the path.

The woman led the children still deeper into the forest, where they had never in their lives been before. Then a great fire was again made, and the mother said: 'Just sit there, you children, and when you are tired you may sleep a little; we are going into the forest to cut wood, and in the evening when we are done, we will come and fetch you away.'

When it was noon, Gretel shared her piece of bread with Hansel, who had scattered his by the way. Then they fell asleep and evening passed, but no one came to the poor children. They did not awake until it was dark night, and Hansel comforted his little sister and said: 'Just wait, Gretel, until the moon rises, and then we shall see the crumbs of bread which I have strewn about. They will show us our way home again.'

When the moon came they set out, but they found no crumbs, for the many thousands of birds which fly about in the woods and fields had picked them all up. Hansel said to Gretel: 'We shall soon find the way,' but they did not find it. They walked the whole night and all the next day too from morning till evening, but they did not get out of the forest, and were very hungry, for they had nothing to eat but two or three berries, which grew on the ground. And as they were so weary that their legs would carry them no longer, they lay down beneath a tree and fell asleep.

It was now three mornings since they had left their father's house. They began to walk again, but they always came deeper into the forest, and if help did not come soon, they must die of hunger and weariness.

When it was mid-day, they saw a beautiful snow-white bird sitting on a bough, which sang so delightfully that they stood still and listened to it. And when its song was over, it spread its wings and flew away before them, and they followed it until they reached a little house, on the roof of which it alighted; and when they approached the little house, they saw that it was built of bread and covered with cakes, but that the windows were of clear sugar.

'We will set to work on that,' said Hansel, 'and have a good meal. I will eat a bit of the roof, and you Gretel, can eat some of the window, it will taste sweet.' Hansel reached up above, and broke off a little of the roof to try how it tasted, and Gretel leant against the window and nibbled at the panes. Then a soft voice cried from the parlour:

'Nibble, nibble, gnaw, Who is nibbling at my little house?'

The children answered:

The wind, the wind,
The heaven-born wind,

And went on eating without disturbing themselves. Hansel, who liked the taste of the roof, tore down a great piece of it, and Gretel pushed out the whole of one round window-pane, sat down, and enjoyed herself. Suddenly the door opened, and a woman as old as the hills, who supported herself on crutches, came creeping out. Hansel and Gretel were so terribly frightened that they let fall what they had in their hands. The old woman, however, nodded her head, and said: 'Oh, you dear children, who has brought you here? Do come in, and stay with me. No harm shall happen to you.' She took them both by the hand, and led them into her little house. Then good food was set before them, milk and pancakes, with sugar, apples, and nuts. Afterwards, two pretty little beds were covered with clean white linen, and Hansel and Gretel lay down in them, and thought they were in heaven.

The old woman had only pretended to be so kind; she was, in reality, a wicked witch, who lay in wait for children, and had only built the little house of bread in order to entice them there. When a child fell into her power, she killed it, cooked and ate it, and that was a feast day with her. Witches have red eyes, and cannot see far, but they have a keen scent like the beasts, and are aware when human beings draw near. When Hansel and Gretel came into her neighbourhood, she laughed with malice, and said mockingly: 'I have them, they shall not escape me again!' Early in the morning before the children were awake, she was already up, and when she saw both of them sleeping and looking so pretty, with their plump and rosy cheeks, she muttered to herself: 'That will be a dainty mouthful!' Then she seized Hansel with her shrivelled hand, carried him into a little stable, and locked him in behind a grated door. Scream as he might, it would not help him. Then she went to Gretel, shook her till she awoke, and cried: 'Get up, lazy thing, fetch some water, and cook something good for your brother; he is in the stable outside, and is to be made fat. When he is fat, I will eat him.' Gretel began to weep bitterly, but it was all in vain, for she was forced to do what the wicked witch commanded.

And now the best food was cooked for poor Hansel, but Gretel got nothing but crab-shells. Every morning, the woman crept to the little stable, and cried: 'Hansel, stretch out your finger that I may feel if you will soon be fat.' Hansel, however, stretched out a little bone to her, and the old woman, who had dim eyes, could not see it, and thought it was Hansel's finger, and was astonished that there was no way of fattening him. When four weeks had gone by, and Hansel still remained thin, she was seized with impatience and would not wait any longer.

'Now, then, Gretel,' she cried to the girl, 'stir yourself, and bring some water. Let Hansel be fat or lean, tomorrow I will kill him, and cook him.' Ah, how the poor little sister did lament when she had to fetch the water, and how her tears did flow down her cheeks!

'Dear God, do help us,' she cried. 'If the wild beasts in the forest had but devoured us, we should at any rate have died together.'

'Just keep your noise to yourself,' said the old woman, 'it won't help you at all.'

Early in the morning, Gretel had to go out and hang up the cauldron with the water, and lit the fire.

'We will bake first,' said the old woman, 'I have already heated the oven, and kneaded the dough.' She pushed poor Gretel out to the oven, from which flames of fire were already darting.

'Creep in,' said the witch, 'and see if it is properly heated, so that we can put the bread in.' And once Gretel was inside, she intended to shut the oven and let her bake in it, and then she would eat her, too. But Gretel saw what she had in mind, and said: 'I do not know how I am to do it; how do I get in?'

'Silly goose,' said the old woman. 'The door is big enough; just look, I can get in myself!' and she crept up and thrust her head into the oven. Then Gretel gave her a push that drove her far into it, and shut the iron door, and fastened the bolt. Oh! then she began to howl quite horribly, but Gretel ran away and the godless witch was miserably burnt to death.

Gretel, however, ran like lightning to Hansel, opened his little stable, and cried: 'Hansel, we are saved! The old witch is dead!'

Then Hansel sprang like a bird from its cage when the door is opened. How they did rejoice and embrace each other, and dance about and kiss each other! And as they had no longer any need to fear her, they went into the witch's house, and in every corner there stood chests full of pearls and jewels.

'These are far better than pebbles!' said Hansel, and thrust into his pockets whatever could be got in, and Gretel said: 'I, too, will take something home with me,' and filled her pinafore full.

'But now we must be off,' said Hansel, 'that we may get out of the witch's forest.'

When they had walked for two hours, they came to a great stretch of water. 'We cannot cross,' said Hansel, 'I see no foot-plank, and no bridge.'

'And there is also no ferry,' answered Gretel, 'but a white duck is swimming there: if I ask her, she will help us over.'

Then she cried:
Little duck, little duck, dost thou see,
Hansel and Gretel are waiting for thee?
There's never a plank, or bridge in sight,
Take us across on thy back so white.

The duck came to them, and Hansel seated himself on its back, and told his sister to sit by him. 'No,' replied Gretel, 'that will be too heavy for the little duck; she shall take us across, one after the other.'

The good little duck did so, and when they were once safely across and had walked for a short time, the forest seemed to be more and more familiar to them, and at length they saw from afar, their father's house. Then they began to run, rushed into the parlour, and threw themselves round their father's neck.

The man had not known one happy hour since he had left the children in the forest; the woman, however, was dead. Gretel emptied her pinafore until pearls and precious stones ran about the room, and Hansel threw one handful after another out of his pocket to add to them. Then all anxiety was at an end, and they lived together in perfect happiness.

My tale is done, there runs a mouse; whosoever catches it, may make himself a big fur cap out of it.

THE SNOW QUEEN IN SEVEN STORIES

Hans Christian Andersen

I. Which deals with the Mirror and its Fragments

You must attend to the commencement of this story, for when we get to the end we shall know more than we do now about a very wicked hobgoblin; he was one of the very worst, for he was a real demon. One day, when he was in a merry mood, he made a looking-glass which had the power of making everything good or beautiful that was reflected in it almost shrink to nothing, while everything that was worthless and bad looked increased in size and worse than ever. The most lovely landscapes appeared like boiled spinach, and the people became hideous, and looked as if they stood on their heads and had no bodies. Their countenances were so distorted that no one could recognise them, and even one freckle on the face appeared to spread over the whole of the nose and mouth. The demon said this was very amusing. When a good or pious thought passed through the mind of any one it was misrepresented in the glass; and then how the demon laughed at his cunning invention. All who went to the demon's school—for he kept a school—talked everywhere of the wonders they had seen, and declared that people could now, for the first time, see what the world and mankind were really like. They carried the glass about everywhere, till at last there was not a land nor a people who had not been looked at through this distorted mirror. They wanted even to fly with it up to heaven to see the angels, but the higher they flew, the more slippery the glass became, and they could scarcely hold it, till at last it slipped from their hands, fell to the earth, and was broken into millions of pieces. But now the looking-glass caused more unhappiness than ever, for some of the fragments were not so large as a grain of sand, and they flew about the world into every country. When one of these tiny atoms flew into a person's eye, it stuck there unknown to him, and from that moment, he saw everything through a distorted medium, or could see only the worst side of what he looked at, for even the smallest fragment retained the same power which had belonged to the whole mirror. Some few persons even got a fragment of the looking-glass in their hearts, and this was very terrible, for their hearts became cold like a lump of ice. A few of the pieces were so large that they could be used as window-panes; it would have been a sad thing to look at our friends through them. Other pieces were made into spectacles; this was dreadful for those who wore them, for they could see nothing either rightly or justly. At all this, the wicked demon laughed till his sides shook—it tickled him so to see the mischief he had done. There were still a number of these little fragments of glass floating about in the air, and now you shall hear what happened with one of them.

***

II. A Little Boy and A Little Girl

In a large town, full of houses and people, there is not room for everybody to have even a little garden, therefore, they are obliged to be satisfied with a few flowers in flower-pots. In one of these large towns lived two poor children who had a garden something larger and better than a few flower-pots. They were not brother and sister, but they loved each other almost as much as if they had been. Their parents lived opposite to each other in two garrets, where the roofs of neighbouring houses projected out towards each other and the water-pipe ran between them. In each house was a little window, so that anyone could step across the gutter from one window to the other. The parents of these children had each a large wooden box in which they cultivated kitchen herbs for their own use, and a little rose-bush in each box, which grew splendidly. Now, after a while, the parents decided to place these two boxes across the water-pipe, so that they reached from one window to the other and looked like two banks of flowers. Sweet-peas drooped over the boxes, and the rose-bushes shot forth long branches, which were trained round the windows and clustered together almost like a triumphal arch of leaves and flowers. The boxes were very high, and the children knew they must not climb upon them, without permission, but they were often, however, allowed to step out together and sit upon their little stools under the rose-bushes, or play quietly. In winter all this pleasure came to an end, for the windows were sometimes quite frozen over. But then they would warm copper pennies on the stove, and hold the warm pennies against the frozen pane; there would be very soon a little round hole through which they could peep, and the soft bright eyes of the little boy and girl would beam through the hole at each window as they looked at each other. Their names were Kay and Gerda. In summer they could be together with one jump from the window, but in winter they had to go up and down the long staircase, and out through the snow before they could meet.

'See there are the white bees swarming,' said Kay's old grandmother one day when it was snowing.

'Have they a queen bee?' asked the little boy, for he knew that the real bees had a queen.

'To be sure they have,' said the grandmother. 'She is flying there where the swarm is thickest. She is the largest of them all, and never remains on the earth, but flies up to the dark clouds. Often at midnight, she flies through the streets of the town, and looks in at the windows, then the ice freezes on the panes into wonderful shapes, that look like flowers and castles.'

'Yes, I have seen them,' said both the children, and they knew it must be true.

'Can the Snow Queen come in here?' asked the little girl.

'Only let her come,' said the boy, 'I'll set her on the stove and then she'll melt.'

Then the grandmother smoothed his hair and told him some more tales. One evening, when little Kay was at home, half undressed, he climbed on a chair by the window and peeped out through the little hole. A few flakes of snow were falling, and one of them, rather larger than the rest, alighted on the edge of one of the flower boxes. This snow-flake grew larger and larger, till at last it became the figure of a woman, dressed in garments of white gauze, which looked like millions of starry snow-flakes linked together. She was fair and beautiful, but made of ice—shining and glittering ice. Still she was alive and her eyes sparkled like bright stars, but there was neither peace nor rest in their glance. She nodded towards the window and waved her hand. The little boy was frightened and sprang from the chair; at the same moment it seemed as if a large bird flew by the window. On the following day there was a clear frost, and very soon came the spring. The sun shone; the young green leaves burst forth; the swallows built their nests; windows were opened, and the children sat once more in the garden on the roof, high above all the other rooms. How beautiful the roses blossomed this summer. The little girl had learnt a hymn in which roses were spoken of, and then she thought of their own roses, and she sang the hymn to the little boy, and he sang too:—

Roses bloom and cease to be,
But we shall the Christ-child see.

Then the little ones held each other by the hand, and kissed the roses, and looked at the bright sunshine, and spoke to it as if the Christ-child were there. Those were splendid summer days. How beautiful and fresh it was out among the rose-bushes, which seemed as if they would never leave off blooming. One day Kay and Gerda sat looking at a book full of pictures of animals and birds, and then just as the clock in the church tower struck twelve, Kay said, 'Oh, something has struck my heart!' and soon after, 'There is something in my eye.'

The little girl put her arm round his neck, and looked into his eye, but she could see nothing.

'I think it is gone,' he said. But it was not gone; it was one of those bits of the looking-glass—that magic mirror, of which we have spoken—the ugly glass which made everything great and good appear small and ugly, while all that was wicked and bad became more visible, and every little fault could be plainly seen. Poor little Kay had also received a small grain in his heart, which very quickly turned to a lump of ice. He felt no more pain, but the glass was there still. 'Why do you cry?' said he at last; 'it makes you look ugly. There is nothing the matter with me now. Oh, see!' he cried suddenly, 'that rose is worm-eaten, and this one is quite crooked. After all they are ugly roses, just like the box in which they stand,' and then he kicked the boxes with his foot, and pulled off the two roses.

'Kay, what are you doing?' cried the little girl; and then, when he saw how frightened she was, he tore off another rose, and jumped through his own window away from little Gerda.

When she afterwards brought out the picture book, he said, 'It was only fit for babies in long clothes,' and when grandmother told any stories, he would interrupt her with 'but;' or, when he could manage it, he would get behind her chair, put on a pair of spectacles, and imitate her very cleverly, to make people laugh. By-and-by he began to mimic the speech and gait of persons in the street. All that was peculiar or disagreeable in a person he would imitate directly, and people said, 'That boy will be very clever; he has a remarkable genius.' But it was the piece of glass in his eye, and the coldness in his heart, that made him act like this. He would even tease little Gerda, who loved him with all her heart. His games, too, were quite different; they were not so childish. One winter's day, when it snowed, he brought out a burning-glass, then he held out the tail of his blue coat, and let the snow-flakes fall upon it. 'Look in this glass, Gerda,' said he; and she saw how every flake of snow was magnified, and looked like a beautiful flower or a glittering star. 'Is it not clever?' said Kay, 'and much more interesting than looking at real flowers. There is not a single fault in it, and the snow-flakes are quite perfect till they begin to melt.'

Soon after Kay made his appearance in large thick gloves, and with his sledge at his back. He called up stairs to Gerda, 'I've got to leave to go into the great square, where the other boys play and ride.' And away he went.

In the great square, the boldest among the boys would often tie their sledges to the country people's carts, and go with them a good way. This was capital. But while they were all amusing themselves, and Kay with them, a great sledge came by; it was painted white, and in it sat some one wrapped in a rough white fur, and wearing a white cap. The sledge drove twice round the square, and Kay fastened his own little sledge to it, so that when it went away, he followed with it. It went faster and faster right through the next street, and then the person who drove turned round and nodded pleasantly to Kay, just as if they were acquainted with each other, but whenever Kay wished to loosen his little sledge the driver nodded again, so Kay sat still, and they drove out through the town gate. Then the snow began to fall so heavily that the little boy could not see a hand's breadth before him, but still they drove on; then he suddenly loosened the cord so that the large sled might go on without him, but it was of no use, his little carriage held fast, and away they went like the wind. Then he called out loudly, but nobody heard him, while the snow beat upon him, and the sledge flew onwards. Every now and then it gave a jump as if it were going over hedges and ditches. The boy was frightened, and tried to say a prayer, but he could remember nothing but the multiplication table.

The snow-flakes became larger and larger, till they appeared like great white chickens. All at once they sprang on one side, the great sledge stopped, and the person who had driven it rose up. The fur and the cap, which were made entirely of snow, fell off, and he saw a lady, tall and white, it was the Snow Queen.

'We have driven well,' said she, 'but why do you tremble? here, creep into my warm fur.' Then she seated him beside her in the sledge, and as she wrapped the fur round him he felt as if he were sinking into a snow drift.

'Are you still cold,' she asked, as she kissed him on the forehead. The kiss was colder than ice; it went quite through to his heart, which was already almost a lump of ice; he felt as if he were going to die, but only for a moment; he soon seemed quite well again, and did not notice the cold around him.

'My sledge! don't forget my sledge,' was his first thought, and then he looked and saw that it was bound fast to one of the white chickens, which flew behind him with the sledge at its back. The Snow Queen kissed little Kay again, and by this time he had forgotten little Gerda, his grandmother, and all at home.

'Now you must have no more kisses,' she said, 'or I should kiss you to death.'

Kay looked at her, and saw that she was so beautiful, he could not imagine a more lovely and intelligent face; she did not now seem to be made of ice, as when he had seen her through his window, and she had nodded to him. In his eyes she was perfect, and she did not feel at all afraid. He told her he could do mental arithmetic, as far as fractions, and that he knew the number of square miles and the number of inhabitants in the country. And she always smiled so that he thought he did not know enough yet, and she looked round the vast expanse as she flew higher and higher with him upon a black cloud, while the storm blew and howled as if it were singing old songs. They flew over woods and lakes, over sea and land; below them roared the wild wind; the wolves howled and the snow crackled; over them flew the black screaming crows, and above all shone the moon, clear and bright—and so Kay passed through the long winter's night, and by day he slept at the feet of the Snow Queen.

***

III. The Flower Garden of the Woman Who Could Conjure

But how fared little Gerda during Kay's absence? What had become of him, no one knew, nor could anyone give the slightest information, excepting the boys, who said that he had tied his sledge to another very large one, which had driven through the street, and out at the town gate. Nobody knew where it went; many tears were shed for him, and little Gerda wept bitterly for a long time. She said she knew he must be dead; that he was drowned in the river which flowed close by the school.

Oh, indeed those long winter days were very dreary. But at last spring came, with warm sunshine. 'Kay is dead and gone,' said little Gerda.

'I don't believe it,' said the sunshine.

'He is dead and gone,' she said to the sparrows.

'We don't believe it,' they replied; and at last little Gerda began to doubt it herself. 'I will put on my new red shoes,' she said one morning, 'those that Kay has never seen, and then I will go down to the river, and ask for him.' It was quite early when she kissed her old grandmother, who was still asleep; then she put on her red shoes, and went quite alone out of the town gates toward the river. 'Is it true that you have taken my little playmate away from me?' said she to the river. 'I will give you my red shoes if you will give him back to me.' And it seemed as if the waves nodded to her in a strange manner. Then she took off her red shoes, which she liked better than anything else, and threw them both into the river, but they fell near the bank, and the little waves carried them back to the land, just as if the river would not take from her what she loved best, because they could not give her back little Kay. But she thought the shoes had not been thrown out far enough. Then she crept into a boat that lay among the reeds, and threw the shoes again from the farther end of the boat into the water, but it was not fastened. And her movement sent it gliding away from the land. When she saw this she hastened to reach the end of the boat, but before she could so it was more than a yard from the bank, and drifting away faster than ever. Then little Gerda was very much frightened, and began to cry, but no one heard her except the sparrows, and they could not carry her to land, but they flew along by the shore, and sang, as if to comfort her, 'Here we are! Here we are!'

The boat floated with the stream; little Gerda sat quite still with only her stockings on her feet; the red shoes floated after her, but she could not reach them because the boat kept so much in advance. The banks on each side of the river were very pretty. There were beautiful flowers, old trees, sloping fields, in which cows and sheep were grazing, but not a man to be seen. Perhaps the river will carry me to little Kay, thought Gerda, and then she became more cheerful, and raised her head, and looked at the beautiful green banks; and so the boat sailed on for hours. At length she came to a large cherry orchard, in which stood a small red house with strange red and blue windows. It had also a thatched roof, and outside were two wooden soldiers, that presented arms to her as she sailed past. Gerda called out to them, for she thought they were alive, but of course they did not answer; and as the boat drifted nearer to the shore, she saw what they really were. Then Gerda called still louder, and there came a very old woman out of the house, leaning on a crutch. She wore a large hat to shade her from the sun, and on it were painted all sorts of pretty flowers. 'You poor little child,' said the old woman, 'how did you manage to come all this distance into the wide world on such a rapid rolling stream?' And then the old woman walked in the water, seized the boat with her crutch, drew it to land, and lifted Gerda out. And Gerda was glad to feel herself on dry ground, although she was rather afraid of the strange old woman. 'Come and tell me who you are,' said she, 'and how came you here.'

Then Gerda told her everything, while the old woman shook her head, and said, 'Hem-hem;' and when she had finished, Gerda asked if she had not seen little Kay, and the old woman told her he had not passed by that way, but he very likely would come. So she told Gerda not to be sorrowful, but to taste the cherries and look at the flowers; they were better than any picture-book, for each of them could tell a story. Then she took Gerda by the hand and led her into the little house, and the old woman closed the door. The windows were very high, and as the panes were red, blue, and yellow, the daylight shone through them in all sorts of singular colors. On the table stood beautiful cherries, and Gerda had permission to eat as many as she would. While she was eating them the old woman combed out her long flaxen ringlets with a golden comb, and the glossy curls hung down on each side of the little round pleasant face, which looked fresh and blooming as a rose. 'I have long been wishing for a dear little maiden like you,' said the old woman, 'and now you must stay with me, and see how happily we shall live together.' And while she went on combing little Gerda's hair, she thought less and less about her adopted brother Kay, for the old woman could conjure, although she was not a wicked witch; she conjured only a little for her own amusement, and now, because she wanted to keep Gerda.

Therefore she went into the garden, and stretched out her crutch towards all the rose-trees, beautiful though they were; and they immediately sunk into the dark earth, so that no one could tell where they had once stood.

The old woman was afraid that if little Gerda saw roses she would think of those at home, and then remember little Kay, and run away. Then she took Gerda into the flower-garden. How fragrant and beautiful it was! Every flower that could be thought of for every season of the year was here in full bloom; no picture-book could have more beautiful colors. Gerda jumped for joy, and played till the sun went down behind the tall cherry-trees; then she slept in an elegant bed with red silk pillows, embroidered with colored violets; and then she dreamed as pleasantly as a queen on her wedding day. The next day, and for many days after, Gerda played with the flowers in the warm sunshine. She knew every flower, and yet, although there were so many of them, it seemed as if one were missing, but which it was she could not tell. One day, however, as she sat looking at the old woman's hat with the painted flowers on it, she saw that the prettiest of them all was a rose. The old woman had forgotten to take it from her hat when she made all the roses sink into the earth. But it is difficult to keep the thoughts together in everything; one little mistake upsets all our arrangements.

'What, are there no roses here?' cried Gerda; and she ran out into the garden, and examined all the beds, and searched and searched. There was not one to be found. Then she sat down and wept, and her tears fell just on the place where one of the rose-trees had sunk down. The warm tears moistened the earth, and the rose-tree sprouted up at once, as blooming as when it had sunk; and Gerda embraced it and kissed the roses, and thought of the beautiful roses at home, and, with them, of little Kay.

'Oh, how I have been detained!' said the little maiden, 'I wanted to seek for little Kay. Do you know where he is?' she asked the roses; 'do you think he is dead?'

And the roses answered, 'No, he is not dead. We have been in the ground where all the dead lie; but Kay is not there.'

'Thank you,' said little Gerda, and then she went to the other flowers, and looked into their little cups, and asked, 'Do you know where little Kay is?' But each flower, as it stood in the sunshine, dreamed only of its own little fairy tale of history. Not one knew anything of Kay. Gerda heard many stories from the flowers, as she asked them one after another about him.

And what, said the tiger-lily? 'Hark, do you hear the drum?—turn, turn,'—there are only two notes, always, 'turn, turn.' Listen to the women's song of mourning! Hear the cry of the priest! In her long red robe stands the Hindoo widow by the funeral pile. The flames rise around her as she places herself on the dead body of her husband; but the Hindoo woman is thinking of the living one in that circle; of him, her son, who lighted those flames. Those shining eyes trouble her heart more painfully than the flames which will soon consume her body to ashes.

Can the fire of the heart be extinguished in the flames of the funeral pile?'

'I don't understand that at all,' said little Gerda.

'That is my story,' said the tiger-lily.

What, says the convolvulus? 'Near yonder narrow road stands an old knight's castle; thick ivy creeps over the old ruined walls, leaf over leaf, even to the balcony, in which stands a beautiful maiden. She bends over the balustrades, and looks up the road. No rose on its stem is fresher than she; no apple-blossom, wafted by the wind, floats more lightly than she moves. Her rich silk rustles as she bends over and exclaims, 'Will he not come?'

'Is it Kay you mean?' asked Gerda.

'I am only speaking of a story of my dream,' replied the flower.

What, said the little snow-drop? 'Between two trees a rope is hanging; there is a piece of board upon it; it is a swing. Two pretty little girls, in dresses white as snow, and with long green ribbons fluttering from their hats, are sitting upon it swinging. Their brother who is taller than they are, stands in the swing; he has one arm round the rope, to steady himself; in one hand he holds a little bowl, and in the other a clay pipe; he is blowing bubbles. As the swing goes on, the bubbles fly upward, reflecting the most beautiful varying colors. The last still hangs from the bowl of the pipe, and sways in the wind. On goes the swing; and then a little black dog comes running up. He is almost as light as the bubble, and he raises himself on his hind legs, and wants to be taken into the swing; but it does not stop, and the dog falls; then he barks and gets angry. The children stoop towards him, and the bubble bursts. A swinging plank, a light sparkling foam picture,—that is my story.'

'It may be all very pretty what you are telling me,' said little Gerda, 'but you speak so mournfully, and you do not mention little Kay at all.'

What do the hyacinths say? 'There were three beautiful sisters, fair and delicate. The dress of one was red, of the second blue, and of the third pure white. Hand in hand they danced in the bright moonlight, by the calm lake; but they were human beings, not fairy elves. The sweet fragrance attracted them, and they disappeared in the wood; here the fragrance became stronger. Three coffins, in which lay the three beautiful maidens, glided from the thickest part of the forest across the lake. The fire-flies flew lightly over them, like little floating torches. Do the dancing maidens sleep, or are they dead? The scent of the flower says that they are corpses. The evening bell tolls their knell.'

'You make me quite sorrowful,' said little Gerda; 'your perfume is so strong, you make me think of the dead maidens. Ah! is little Kay really dead then? The roses have been in the earth, and they say no.'

'Cling, clang,' tolled the hyacinth bells. 'We are not tolling for little Kay; we do not know him. We sing our song, the only one we know.'

Then Gerda went to the buttercups that were glittering amongst the bright green leaves.

'You are little bright suns,' said Gerda; 'tell me if you know where I can find my play-fellow.'

And the buttercups sparkled gayly, and looked again at Gerda. What song could the buttercups sing? It was not about Kay.

'The bright warm sun shone on a little court, on the first warm day of spring. His bright beams rested on the white walls of the neighboring house; and close by bloomed the first yellow flower of the season, glittering like gold in the sun's warm ray. An old woman sat in her arm chair at the house door, and her granddaughter, a poor and pretty servant-maid came to see her for a short visit. When she kissed her grandmother there was gold everywhere: the gold of the heart in that holy kiss; it was a golden morning; there was gold in the beaming sunlight, gold in the leaves of the lowly flower, and on the lips of the maiden. There, that is my story,' said the buttercup.

'My poor old grandmother!' sighed Gerda; 'she is longing to see me, and grieving for me as she did for little Kay; but I shall soon go home now, and take little Kay with me. It is no use asking the flowers; they know only their own songs, and can give me no information.'

And then she tucked up her little dress, that she might run faster, but the narcissus caught her by the leg as she was jumping over it; so she stopped and looked at the tall yellow flower, and said, 'Perhaps you may know something.'

Then she stooped down quite close to the flower, and listened; and what did he say?

'I can see myself, I can see myself,' said the narcissus. 'Oh, how sweet is my perfume! Up in a little room with a bow window, stands a little dancing girl, half undressed; she stands sometimes on one leg, and sometimes on both, and looks as if she would tread the whole world under her feet. She is nothing but a delusion. She is pouring water out of a tea-pot on a piece of stuff which she holds in her hand; it is her bodice. 'Cleanliness is a good thing,' she says. Her white dress hangs on a peg; it has also been washed in the tea-pot, and dried on the roof. She puts it on, and ties a saffron-colored handkerchief round her neck, which makes the dress look whiter. See how she stretches out her legs, as if she were showing off on a stem. I can see myself, I can see myself.'

'What do I care for all that,' said Gerda, 'you need not tell me such stuff.' And then she ran to the other end of the garden. The door was fastened, but she pressed against the rusty latch, and it gave way. The door sprang open, and little Gerda ran out with bare feet into the wide world. She looked back three times, but no one seemed to be following her. At last she could run no longer, so she sat down to rest on a great stone, and when she looked round she saw that the summer was over, and autumn very far advanced. She had known nothing of this in the beautiful garden, where the sun shone and the flowers grew all the year round.

'Oh, how I have wasted my time?' said little Gerda; 'it is autumn. I must not rest any longer,' and she rose up to go on. But her little feet were wounded and sore, and everything around her looked so cold and bleak. The long willow-leaves were quite yellow. The dew-drops fell like water, leaf after leaf dropped from the trees, the sloe-thorn alone still bore fruit, but the sloes were sour, and set the teeth on edge. Oh, how dark and weary the whole world appeared!

***

IV. The Prince and Princess

Gerda was obliged to rest again, and just opposite the place where she sat, she saw a great crow come hopping across the snow toward her. He stood looking at her for some time, and then he wagged his head and said, 'Caw, caw; good-day, good-day.' He pronounced the words as plainly as he could, because he meant to be kind to the little girl; and then he asked her where she was going all alone in the wide world.

The word alone Gerda understood very well, and knew how much it expressed. So then she told the crow the whole story of her life and adventures, and asked him if he had seen little Kay.

The crow nodded his head very gravely, and said, 'Perhaps I have—it may be.'

'No! Do you think you have?' cried little Gerda, and she kissed the crow, and hugged him almost to death with joy.

'Gently, gently,' said the crow. 'I believe I know. I think it may be little Kay; but he has certainly forgotten you by this time for the princess.'

'Does he live with a princess?' asked Gerda.

'Yes, listen,' replied the crow, 'but it is so difficult to speak your language. If you understand the crows' language then I can explain it better. Do you?'

'No, I have never learnt it,' said Gerda, 'but my grandmother understands it, and used to speak it to me. I wish I had learnt it.'

'It does not matter,' answered the crow; 'I will explain as well as I can, although it will be very badly done;' and he told her what he had heard. 'In this kingdom where we now are,' said he, 'there lives a princess, who is so wonderfully clever that she has read all the newspapers in the world, and forgotten them too, although she is so clever. A short time ago, as she was sitting on her throne, which people say is not such an agreeable seat as is often supposed, she began to sing a song which commences in these words:

Why should I not be married?

'Why not indeed?' said she, and so she determined to marry if she could find a husband who knew what to say when he was spoken to, and not one who could only look grand, for that was so tiresome. Then she assembled all her court ladies together at the beat of the drum, and when they heard of her intentions they were very much pleased. 'We are so glad to hear it,' said they, we were talking about it ourselves the other day.' You may believe that every word I tell you is true,' said the crow, 'for I have a tame sweetheart who goes freely about the palace, and she told me all this.'

Of course his sweetheart was a crow, for 'birds of a feather flock together,' and one crow always chooses another crow.

'Newspapers were published immediately, with a border of hearts, and the initials of the princess among them. They gave notice that every young man who was handsome was free to visit the castle and speak with the princess; and those who could reply loud enough to be heard when spoken to, were to make themselves quite at home at the palace; but the one who spoke best would be chosen as a husband for the princess. Yes, yes, you may believe me, it is all as true as I sit here,' said the crow. 'The people came in crowds. There was a great deal of crushing and running about, but no one succeeded either on the first or second day. They could all speak very well while they were outside in the streets, but when they entered the palace gates, and saw the guards in silver uniforms, and the footmen in their golden livery on the staircase, and the great halls lighted up, they became quite confused. And when they stood before the throne on which the princess sat, they could do nothing but repeat the last words she had said; and she had no particular wish to hear her own words over again. It was just as if they had all taken something to make them sleepy while they were in the palace, for they did not recover themselves nor speak till they got back again into the street. There was quite a long line of them reaching from the town-gate to the palace. I went myself to see them,' said the crow.

'They were hungry and thirsty, for at the palace they did not get even a glass of water. Some of the wisest had taken a few slices of bread and butter with them, but they did not share it with their neighbors; they thought if they went in to the princess looking hungry, there would be a better chance for themselves.'

'But Kay! tell me about little Kay!' said Gerda, 'was he amongst the crowd?'

'Stop a bit, we are just coming to him. It was on the third day, there came marching cheerfully along to the palace a little personage, without horses or carriage, his eyes sparkling like yours; he had beautiful long hair, but his clothes were very poor.'

'That was Kay!' said Gerda joyfully. 'Oh, then I have found him;' and she clapped her hands.

'He had a little knapsack on his back,' added the crow.

'No, it must have been his sledge,' said Gerda; 'for he went away with it.'

'It may have been so,' said the crow; 'I did not look at it very closely. But I know from my tame sweetheart that he passed through the palace gates, saw the guards in their silver uniform, and the servants in their liveries of gold on the stairs, but he was not in the least embarrassed. 'It must be very tiresome to stand on the stairs,' he said. 'I prefer to go in.' The rooms were blazing with light. Councillors and ambassadors walked about with bare feet, carrying golden vessels; it was enough to make any one feel serious. His boots creaked loudly as he walked, and yet he was not at all uneasy.

'It must be Kay,' said Gerda, 'I know he had new boots on, I have heard them creak in grandmother's room.'

'They really did creak,' said the crow, 'yet he went boldly up to the princess herself, who was sitting on a pearl as large as a spinning wheel, and all the ladies of the court were present with their maids, and all the cavaliers with their servants; and each of the maids had another maid to wait upon her, and the cavaliers' servants had their own servants, as well as a page each. They all stood in circles round the princess, and the nearer they stood to the door, the prouder they looked. The servants' pages, who always wore slippers, could hardly be looked at, they held themselves up so proudly by the door.'

'It must be quite awful,' said little Gerda, 'but did Kay win the princess?'

'If I had not been a crow,' said he, 'I would have married her myself, although I am engaged. He spoke just as well as I do, when I speak the crows' language, so I heard from my tame sweetheart. He was quite free and agreeable and said he had not come to woo the princess, but to hear her wisdom; and he was as pleased with her as she was with him.'

'Oh, certainly that was Kay,' said Gerda, 'he was so clever; he could work mental arithmetic and fractions. Oh, will you take me to the palace?'

'It is very easy to ask that,' replied the crow, 'but how are we to manage it? However, I will speak about it to my tame sweetheart, and ask her advice; for I must tell you it will be very difficult to gain permission for a little girl like you to enter the palace.'

'Oh, yes; but I shall gain permission easily,' said Gerda, 'for when Kay hears that I am here, he will come out and fetch me in immediately.'

'Wait for me here by the palings,' said the crow, wagging his head as he flew away.

It was late in the evening before the crow returned. 'Caw, caw,' he said, 'she sends you greeting, and here is a little roll which she took from the kitchen for you; there is plenty of bread there, and she thinks you must be hungry. It is not possible for you to enter the palace by the front entrance. The guards in silver uniform and the servants in gold livery would not allow it. But do not cry, we will manage to get you in; my sweetheart knows a little back-staircase that leads to the sleeping apartments, and she knows where to find the key.'

Then they went into the garden through the great avenue, where the leaves were falling one after another, and they could see the light in the palace being put out in the same manner. And the crow led little Gerda to the back door, which stood ajar. Oh! how little Gerda's heart beat with anxiety and longing; it was just as if she were going to do something wrong, and yet she only wanted to know where little Kay was. 'It must be he,' she thought, 'with those clear eyes, and that long hair.' She could fancy she saw him smiling at her, as he used to at home, when they sat among the roses. He would certainly be glad to see her, and to hear what a long distance she had come for his sake, and to know how sorry they had been at home because he did not come back. Oh what joy and yet fear she felt! They were now on the stairs, and in a small closet at the top a lamp was burning. In the middle of the floor stood the tame crow, turning her head from side to side, and gazing at Gerda, who curtseyed as her grandmother had taught her to do.

'My betrothed has spoken so very highly of you, my little lady,' said the tame crow, 'your life-history, Vita, as it may be called, is very touching. If you will take the lamp I will walk before you. We will go straight along this way, then we shall meet no one.'

'It seems to me as if somebody were behind us,' said Gerda, as something rushed by her like a shadow on the wall, and then horses with flying manes and thin legs, hunters, ladies and gentlemen on horseback, glided by her, like shadows on the wall.

'They are only dreams,' said the crow, 'they are coming to fetch the thoughts of the great people out hunting.'

'All the better, for we shall be able to look at them in their beds more safely. I hope that when you rise to honor and favor, you will show a grateful heart.'

'You may be quite sure of that,' said the crow from the forest.

They now came into the first hall, the walls of which were hung with rose-colored satin, embroidered with artificial flowers. Here the dreams again flitted by them but so quickly that Gerda could not distinguish the royal persons. Each hall appeared more splendid than the last, it was enought to bewilder any one. At length they reached a bedroom. The ceiling was like a great palm-tree, with glass leaves of the most costly crystal, and over the centre of the floor two beds, each resembling a lily, hung from a stem of gold. One, in which the princess lay, was white, the other was red; and in this Gerda had to seek for little Kay. She pushed one of the red leaves aside, and saw a little brown neck. Oh, that must be Kay! She called his name out quite loud, and held the lamp over him. The dreams rushed back into the room on horseback. He woke, and turned his head round, it was not little Kay! The prince was only like him in the neck, still he was young and pretty. Then the princess peeped out of her white-lily bed, and asked what was the matter. Then little Gerda wept and told her story, and all that the crows had done to help her.

'You poor child,' said the prince and princess; then they praised the crows, and said they were not angry for what they had done, but that it must not happen again, and this time they should be rewarded.

'Would you like to have your freedom?' asked the princess, 'or would you prefer to be raised to the position of court crows, with all that is left in the kitchen for yourselves?'

Then both the crows bowed, and begged to have a fixed appointment, for they thought of their old age, and said it would be so comfortable to feel that they had provision for their old days, as they called it. And then the prince got out of his bed, and gave it up to Gerda,—he could do no more; and she lay down. She folded her little hands, and thought, 'How good everyone is to me, men and animals too;' then she closed her eyes and fell into a sweet sleep. All the dreams came flying back again to her, and they looked like angels, and one of them drew a little sledge, on which sat Kay, and nodded to her. But all this was only a dream, and vanished as soon as she awoke.

The following day she was dressed from head to foot in silk and velvet, and they invited her to stay at the palace for a few days, and enjoy herself, but she only begged for a pair of boots, and a little carriage, and a horse to draw it, so that she might go into the wide world to seek for Kay. And she obtained, not only boots, but also a muff, and she was neatly dressed; and when she was ready to go, there, at the door, she found a coach made of pure gold, with the coat-of-arms of the prince and princess shining upon it like a star, and the coachman, footman, and outriders all wearing golden crowns on their heads. The prince and princess themselves helped her into the coach, and wished her success. The forest crow, who was now married, accompanied her for the first three miles; he sat by Gerda's side, as he could not bear riding backwards. The tame crow stood in the doorway flapping her wings. She could not go with them, because she had been suffering from headache ever since the new appointment, no doubt from eating too much. The coach was well stored with sweet cakes, and under the seat were fruit and gingerbread nuts. 'Farewell, farewell,' cried the prince and princess, and little Gerda wept, and the crow wept; and then, after a few miles, the crow also said 'Farewell,' and this was the saddest parting. However, he flew to a tree, and stood flapping his black wings as long as he could see the coach, which glittered in the bright sunshine.

***

V. Little Robber-Girl

The coach drove on through a thick forest, where it lighted up the way like a torch, and dazzled the eyes of some robbers, who could not bear to let it pass them unmolested.

'It is gold! it is gold!' cried they, rushing forward, and seizing the horses. Then they struck the little jockeys, the coachman, and the footman dead, and pulled little Gerda out of the carriage.

'She is fat and pretty, and she has been fed with the kernels of nuts,' said the old robber-woman, who had a long beard and eyebrows that hung over her eyes. 'She is as good as a little lamb; how nice she will taste!' and as she said this, she drew forth a shining knife, that glittered horribly. 'Oh!' screamed the old woman the same moment; for her own daughter, who held her back, had bitten her in the ear. She was a wild and naughty girl, and the mother called her an ugly thing, and had not time to kill Gerda.

'She shall play with me,' said the little robber-girl; 'she shall give me her muff and her pretty dress, and sleep with me in my bed.' And then she bit her mother again, and made her spring in the air, and jump about; and all the robbers laughed, and said, 'See how she is dancing with her young cub.'

'I will have a ride in the coach,' said the little robber-girl; and she would have her own way; for she was so self-willed and obstinate.

She and Gerda seated themselves in the coach, and drove away, over stumps and stones, into the depths of the forest. The little robber-girl was about the same size as Gerda, but stronger; she had broader shoulders and a darker skin; her eyes were quite black, and she had a mournful look. She clasped little Gerda round the waist, and said,—

'They shall not kill you as long as you don't make us vexed with you. I suppose you are a princess.'

'No,' said Gerda; and then she told her all her history, and how fond she was of little Kay.

The robber-girl looked earnestly at her, nodded her head slightly, and said, 'They sha'nt kill you, even if I do get angry with you; for I will do it myself.' And then she wiped Gerda's eyes, and stuck her own hands in the beautiful muff which was so soft and warm.

The coach stopped in the courtyard of a robber's castle, the walls of which were cracked from top to bottom. Ravens and crows flew in and out of the holes and crevices, while great bulldogs, either of which looked as if it could swallow a man, were jumping about; but they were not allowed to bark. In the large and smoky hall a bright fire was burning on the stone floor. There was no chimney; so the smoke went up to the ceiling, and found a way out for itself. Soup was boiling in a large cauldron, and hares and rabbits were roasting on the spit.

'You shall sleep with me and all my little animals to-night,' said the robber-girl, after they had had something to eat and drink. So she took Gerda to a corner of the hall, where some straw and carpets were laid down. Above them, on laths and perches, were more than a hundred pigeons, who all seemed to be asleep, although they moved slightly when the two little girls came near them. 'These all belong to me,' said the robber-girl; and she seized the nearest to her, held it by the feet, and shook it till it flapped its wings. 'Kiss it,' cried she, flapping it in Gerda's face. 'There sit the wood-pigeons,' continued she, pointing to a number of laths and a cage which had been fixed into the walls, near one of the openings. 'Both rascals would fly away directly, if they were not closely locked up. And here is my old sweetheart 'Ba;' and she dragged out a reindeer by the horn; he wore a bright copper ring round his neck, and was tied up. 'We are obliged to hold him tight too, or else he would run away from us also. I tickle his neck every evening with my sharp knife, which frightens him very much.' And then the robber-girl drew a long knife from a chink in the wall, and let it slide gently over the reindeer's neck. The poor animal began to kick, and the little robber-girl laughed, and pulled down Gerda into bed with her.

'Will you have that knife with you while you are asleep?' asked Gerda, looking at it in great fright.

'I always sleep with the knife by me,' said the

robber-girl. 'No one knows what may happen. But now tell me again all about little Kay, and why you went out into the world.'

Then Gerda repeated her story over again, while the wood-pigeons in the cage over her cooed, and the other pigeons slept. The little robber-girl put one arm across Gerda's neck, and held the knife in the other, and was soon fast asleep and snoring. But Gerda could not close her eyes at all; she knew not whether she was to live or die. The robbers sat round the fire, singing and drinking, and the old woman stumbled about. It was a terrible sight for a little girl to witness.

Then the wood-pigeons said, 'Coo, coo; we have seen little Kay. A white fowl carried his sledge, and he sat in the carriage of the Snow Queen, which drove through the wood while we were lying in our nest. She blew upon us, and all the young ones died excepting us two. Coo, coo.'

'What are you saying up there?' cried Gerda. 'Where was the Snow Queen going? Do you know anything about it?'

'She was most likely travelling to Lapland, where there is always snow and ice. Ask the reindeer that is fastened up there with a rope.'

'Yes, there is always snow and ice,' said the reindeer; 'and it is a glorious place; you can leap and run about freely on the sparkling ice plains. The Snow Queen has her summer tent there, but her strong castle is at the North Pole, on an island called Spitzbergen.'

'Oh, Kay, little Kay!' sighed Gerda.

'Lie still,' said the robber-girl, 'or I shall run my knife into your body.'

In the morning Gerda told her all that the wood-pigeons had said; and the little robber-girl looked quite serious, and nodded her head, and said, 'That is all talk, that is all talk. Do you know where Lapland is?' she asked the reindeer.

'Who should know better than I do?' said the animal, while his eyes sparkled. 'I was born and brought up there, and used to run about the snow-covered plains.'

'Now listen,' said the robber-girl; 'all our men are gone away,—only mother is here, and here she will stay; but at noon she always drinks out of a great bottle, and afterwards sleeps for a little while; and then, I'll do something for you.' Then she jumped out of bed, clasped her mother round the neck, and pulled her by the beard, crying, 'My own little nanny goat, good morning.' Then her mother filliped her nose till it was quite red; yet she did it all for love.

When the mother had drunk out of the bottle, and was gone to sleep, the little robber-maiden went to the reindeer, and said, 'I should like very much to tickle your neck a few times more with my knife, for it makes you look so funny; but never mind,—I will untie your cord, and set you free, so that you may run away to Lapland; but you must make good use of your legs, and carry this little maiden to the castle of the Snow Queen, where her play-fellow is. You have heard what she told me, for she spoke loud enough, and you were listening.'

Then the reindeer jumped for joy; and the little robber-girl lifted Gerda on his back, and had the forethought to tie her on, and even to give her her own little cushion to sit on.

'Here are your fur boots for you,' said she; 'for it will be very cold; but I must keep the muff; it is so pretty. However, you shall not be frozen for the want of it; here are my mother's large warm mittens; they will reach up to your elbows. Let me put them on. There, now your hands look just like my mother's.'

But Gerda wept for joy.

'I don't like to see you fret,' said the little robber-girl; 'you ought to look quite happy now; and here are two loaves and a ham, so that you need not starve.' These were fastened on the reindeer, and then the little robber-maiden opened the door, coaxed in all the great dogs, and then cut the string with which the reindeer was fastened, with her sharp knife, and said, 'Now run, but mind you take good care of the little girl.' And then Gerda stretched out her hand, with the great mitten on it, towards the little robber-girl, and said, 'Farewell,' and away flew the reindeer, over stumps and stones, through the great forest, over marshes and plains, as quickly as he could. The wolves howled, and the ravens screamed; while up in the sky quivered red lights like flames of fire. 'There are my old northern lights,' said the reindeer; 'see how they flash.' And he ran on day and night still faster and faster, but the loaves and the ham were all eaten by the time they reached Lapland.

VI. The Lapland Woman and The Finland Woman

They stopped at a little hut; it was very mean looking; the roof sloped nearly down to the ground, and the door was so low that the family had to creep in on their hands and knees, when they went in and out. There was no one at home but an old Lapland woman, who was cooking fish by the light of a train-oil lamp. The reindeer told her all about Gerda's story, after having first told his own, which seemed to him the most important, but Gerda was so pinched with the cold that she could not speak. 'Oh, you poor things,' said the Lapland woman, 'you have a long way to go yet. You must travel more than a hundred miles farther, to Finland. The Snow Queen lives there now, and she burns Bengal lights every evening. I will write a few words on a dried stock-fish, for I have no paper, and you can take it from me to the Finland woman who lives there; she can give you better information than I can.' So when Gerda was warmed, and had taken something to eat and drink, the woman wrote a few words on the dried fish, and told Gerda to take great care of it. Then she tied her again on the reindeer, and he set off at full speed. Flash, flash, went the beautiful blue northern lights in the air the whole night long. And at length they reached Finland, and knocked at the chimney of the Finland woman's hut, for it had no door above the ground. They crept in, but it was so terribly hot inside that that woman wore scarcely any clothes; she was small and very dirty looking. She loosened little Gerda's dress, and took off the fur boots and the mittens, or Gerda would have been unable to bear the heat; and then she placed a piece of ice on the reindeer's head, and read what was written on the dried fish. After she had read it three times, she knew it by heart, so she popped the fish into the soup saucepan, as she knew it was good to eat, and she never wasted anything. The reindeer told his own story first, and then little Gerda's, and the Finlander twinkled with her clever eyes, but she said nothing. 'You are so clever,' said the reindeer; 'I know you can tie all the winds of the world with a piece of twine. If a sailor unties one knot, he has a fair wind; when he unties the second, it blows hard; but if the third and fourth are loosened, then comes a storm, which will root up whole forests. Cannot you give this little maiden something which will make her as strong as twelve men, to overcome the Snow Queen?'

'The Power of twelve men!' said the Finland woman; 'that would be of very little use.' But she went to a shelf and took down and unrolled a large skin, on which were inscribed wonderful characters, and she read till the perspiration ran down from her forehead. But the reindeer begged so hard for little Gerda, and Gerda looked at the Finland woman with such beseeching tearful eyes, that her own eyes began to twinkle again; so she drew the reindeer into a corner, and whispered to him while she laid a fresh piece of ice on his head, 'Little Kay is really with the Snow Queen, but he finds everything there so much to his taste and his liking, that he believes it is the finest place in the world; but this is because he has a piece of broken glass in his heart, and a little piece of glass in his eye. These must be taken out, or he will never be a human being again, and the Snow Queen will retain her power over him.'

'But can you not give little Gerda something to help her to conquer this power?'

'I can give her no greater power than she has already,' said the woman; 'don't you see how strong that is? How men and animals are obliged to serve her, and how well she has got through the world, barefooted as she is. She cannot receive any power from me greater than she now has, which consists in her own purity and innocence of heart. If she cannot herself obtain access to the Snow Queen, and remove the glass fragments from little Kay, we can do nothing to help her. Two miles from here the Snow Queen's garden begins; you can carry the little girl so far, and set her down by the large bush which stands in the snow, covered with red berries. Do not stay gossiping, but come back here as quickly as you can.' Then the Finland woman lifted little Gerda upon the reindeer, and he ran away with her as quickly as he could.

'Oh, I have forgotten my boots and my mittens,' cried little Gerda, as soon as she felt the cutting cold, but the reindeer dared not stop, so he ran on till he reached the bush with the red berries; here he set Gerda down, and he kissed her, and the great bright tears trickled over the animal's cheeks; then he left her and ran back as fast as he could.

There stood poor Gerda, without shoes, without gloves, in the midst of cold, dreary, ice-bound Finland.

She ran forwards as quickly as she could, when a whole regiment of snow-flakes came round her; they did not, however, fall from the sky, which was quite clear and glittering with the northern lights. The snow-flakes ran along the ground, and the nearer they came to her, the larger they appeared. Gerda remembered how large and beautiful they looked through the burning-glass. But these were really larger, and much more terrible, for they were alive, and were the guards of the Snow Queen, and had the strangest shapes. Some were like great porcupines, others like twisted serpents with their heads stretching out, and some few were like little fat bears with their hair bristled; but all were dazzlingly white, and all were living snow-flakes.

Then little Gerda repeated the Lord's Prayer, and the cold was so great that she could see her own breath come out of her mouth like steam as she uttered the words. The steam appeared to increase, as she continued her prayer, till it took the shape of little angels who grew larger the moment they touched the earth. They all wore helmets on their heads, and carried spears and shields. Their number continued to increase more and more; and by the time Gerda had finished her prayers, a whole legion stood round her. They thrust their spears into the terrible snow-flakes, so that they shivered into a hundred pieces, and little Gerda could go forward with courage and safety. The angels stroked her hands and feet, so that she felt the cold less, and she hastened on to the Snow Queen's castle.

But now we must see what Kay is doing. In truth he thought not of little Gerda, and never supposed she could be standing in the front of the palace.

***

VII. Of the Palace of the Snow Queen and What Happened There at Last

The walls of the palace were formed of drifted snow, and the windows and doors of the cutting winds. There were more than a hundred rooms in it, all as if they had been formed with snow blown together. The largest of them extended for several miles; they were all lighted up by the vivid light of the aurora, and they were so large and empty, so icy cold and glittering! There were no amusements here, not even a little bear's ball, when the storm might have been the music, and the bears could have danced on their hind legs, and shown their good manners. There were no pleasant games of snap-dragon, or touch, or even a gossip over the tea-table, for the young-lady foxes. Empty, vast, and cold were the halls of the Snow Queen. The flickering flame of the northern lights could be plainly seen, whether they rose high or low in the heavens, from every part of the castle. In the midst of its empty, endless hall of snow was a frozen lake, broken on its surface into a thousand forms; each piece resembled another, from being in itself perfect as a work of art, and in the centre of this lake sat the Snow Queen, when she was at home. She called the lake 'The Mirror of Reason,' and said that it was the best, and indeed the only one in the world.

Little Kay was quite blue with cold, indeed almost black, but he did not feel it; for the Snow Queen had kissed away the icy shiverings, and his heart was already a lump of ice. He dragged some sharp, flat pieces of ice to and fro, and placed them together in all kinds of positions, as if he wished to make something out of them; just as we try to form various figures with little tablets of wood which we call 'a Chinese puzzle.' Kay's fingers were very artistic; it was the icy game of reason at which he played, and in his eyes the figures were very remarkable, and of the highest importance; this opinion was owing to the piece of glass still sticking in his eye. He composed many complete figures, forming different words, but there was one word he never could manage to form, although he wished it very much. It was the word 'Eternity.' The Snow Queen had said to him, 'When you can find out this, you shall be your own master, and I will give you the whole world and a new pair of skates.' But he could not accomplish it.

'Now I must hasten away to warmer countries,' said the Snow Queen. 'I will go and look into the black craters of the tops of the burning mountains, Etna and Vesuvius, as they are called,—I shall make them look white, which will be good for them, and for the lemons and the grapes.' And away flew the Snow Queen, leaving little Kay quite alone in the great hall which was so many miles in length; so he sat and looked at his pieces of ice, and was thinking so deeply, and sat so still, that any one might have supposed he was frozen.

Just at this moment it happened that little Gerda came through the great door of the castle. Cutting winds were raging around her, but she offered up a prayer and the winds sank down as if they were going to sleep; and she went on till she came to the large empty hall, and caught sight of Kay; she knew him directly; she flew to him and threw her arms round his neck, and held him fast, while she exclaimed, 'Kay, dear little Kay, I have found you at last.'

But he sat quite still, stiff and cold.

Then little Gerda wept hot tears, which fell on his breast, and penetrated into his heart, and thawed the lump of ice, and washed away the little piece of glass which had stuck there. Then he looked at her, and she sang—

Roses bloom and cease to be,
But we shall the Christ-child see.

Then Kay burst into tears, and he wept so that the splinter of glass swam out of his eye. Then he recognised Gerda, and said, joyfully, 'Gerda, dear little Gerda, where have you been all this time, and where have I been?' And he looked all around him, and said, 'How cold it is, and how large and empty it all looks,' and he clung to Gerda, and she laughed and wept for joy. It was so pleasing to see them that the pieces of ice even danced about; and when they were tired and went to lie down, they formed themselves into the letters of the word which the Snow

Queen had said he must find out before he could be his own master, and have the whole world and a pair of new skates. Then Gerda kissed his cheeks, and they became blooming; and she kissed his eyes, and they shone like her own; she kissed his hands and his feet, and then he became quite healthy and cheerful. The Snow Queen might come home now when she pleased, for there stood his certainty of freedom, in the word she wanted, written in shining letters of ice.

Then they took each other by the hand, and went forth from the great palace of ice. They spoke of the grandmother, and of the roses on the roof, and as they went on the winds were at rest, and the sun burst forth. When they arrived at the bush with red berries, there stood the reindeer waiting for them, and he had brought another young reindeer with him, whose udders were full, and the children drank her warm milk and kissed her on the mouth. Then they carried Kay and Gerda first to the Finland woman, where they warmed themselves thoroughly in the hot room, and she gave them directions about their journey home. Next they went to the Lapland woman, who had made some new clothes for them, and put their sleighs in order. Both the reindeer ran by their side, and followed them as far as the boundaries of the country, where the first green leaves were budding. And here they took leave of the two reindeer and the Lapland woman, and all said—Farewell. Then the birds began to twitter, and the forest too was full of green young leaves; and out of it came a beautiful horse, which Gerda remembered, for it was one which had drawn the golden coach. A young girl was riding upon it, with a shining red cap on her head, and pistols in her belt. It was the little robber-maiden, who had got tired of staying at home; she was going first to the north, and if that did not suit her, she meant to try some other part of the world. She knew Gerda directly, and Gerda remembered her: it was a joyful meeting.

'You are a fine fellow to go gadding about in this way,' said she to little Kay, 'I should like to know whether you deserve that any one should go to the end of the world to find you.'

But Gerda patted her cheeks, and asked after the prince and princess.

'They are gone to foreign countries,' said the robber-girl.

'And the crow?' asked Gerda.

'Oh, the crow is dead,' she replied; 'his tame sweetheart is now a widow, and wears a bit of black worsted round her leg. She mourns very pitifully, but it is all stuff. But now tell me how you managed to get him back.'

Then Gerda and Kay told her all about it.

'Snip, snap, snare! it's all right at last,' said the robber-girl.

Then she took both their hands, and promised that if ever she should pass through the town, she would call and pay them a visit. And then she rode away into the wide world. But Gerda and Kay went hand-in-hand towards home; and as they advanced, spring appeared more lovely with its green verdure and its beautiful flowers. Very soon they recognised the large town where they lived, and the tall steeples of the churches, in which the sweet bells were ringing a merry peal as they entered it, and found their way to their grandmother's door. They went upstairs into the little room, where all looked just as it used to do. The old clock was going 'tick, tick,' and the hands pointed to the time of day, but as they passed through the door into the room they perceived that they were both grown up, and become a man and woman. The roses out on the roof were in full bloom, and peeped in at the window; and there stood the little chairs, on which they had sat when children; and Kay and Gerda seated themselves each on their own chair, and held each other by the hand, while the cold empty grandeur of the Snow Queen's palace vanished from their memories like a painful dream. The grandmother sat in God's bright sunshine, and she read aloud from the Bible, 'Except ye become as little children, ye shall in no wise enter into the kingdom of God.' And Kay and Gerda looked into each other's eyes, and all at once understood the words of the old song,

'Roses bloom and cease to be, But we shall the Christ-child see.'

And they both sat there, grown up, yet children at heart; and it was summer—warm, beautiful summer.

THE BRAVE TIN SOLDIER

Hans Christian Andersen

There were once five-and-twenty tin soldiers, who were all brothers, for they had been made out of the same old tin spoon. They shouldered arms and looked straight before them, and wore a splendid uniform, red and blue. The first thing in the world they ever heard were the words, 'Tin soldiers!' uttered by a little boy, who clapped his hands with delight when the lid of the box, in which they lay, was taken off. They were given him for a birthday present, and he stood at the table to set them up. The soldiers were all exactly alike, excepting one, who had only one leg; he had been left to the last, and then there was not enough of the melted tin to finish him, so they made him to stand firmly on one leg, and this caused him to be very remarkable.

The table on which the tin soldiers stood, was

covered with other playthings, but the most attractive to the eye was a pretty little paper castle. Through the small windows the rooms could be seen. In front of the castle a number of little trees surrounded a piece of looking-glass, which was intended to represent a transparent lake. Swans, made of wax, swam on the lake, and were reflected in it. All this was very pretty, but the prettiest of all was a tiny little lady, who stood at the open door of the castle; she, also, was made of paper, and she wore a dress of clear muslin, with a narrow blue ribbon over her shoulders just like a scarf. In front of these was fixed a glittering tinsel rose, as large as her whole face. The little lady was a dancer, and she stretched out both her arms, and raised one of her legs so high, that the tin soldier could not see it at all, and he thought that she, like himself, had only one leg. 'That is the wife for me,' he thought; 'but she is too grand, and lives in a castle, while I have only a box to live in, five-and-twenty of us altogether, that is no place for her. Still I must try and make her acquaintance.' Then he laid himself at full length on the table behind a snuff-box that stood upon it, so that he could peep at the little delicate lady, who continued to stand on one leg without losing her balance. When evening came, the other tin soldiers were all placed in the box, and the people of the house went to bed. Then the playthings began to have their own games together, to pay visits, to have sham fights, and to give balls. The tin soldiers rattled in their box; they wanted to get out and join the amusements, but they could not open the lid. The nutcrackers played at leap-frog, and the pencil jumped about the table. There was such a noise that the canary woke up and began to talk, and in poetry too. Only the tin soldier and the dancer remained in their places. She stood on tiptoe, with her legs stretched out, as firmly as he did on his one leg. He never took his eyes from her for even a moment. The clock struck twelve, and, with a bounce, up sprang the lid of the snuff-box; but, instead of snuff, there jumped up a little black goblin; for the snuff-box was a toy puzzle.

'Tin soldier,' said the goblin, 'don't wish for what does not belong to you.'

But the tin soldier pretended not to hear.

'Very well; wait till to-morrow, then,' said the goblin.

When the children came in the next morning, they placed the tin soldier in the window. Now, whether it was the goblin who did it, or the draught, is not known, but the window flew open, and out fell the tin soldier, heels over head, from the third story, into the street beneath. It was a terrible fall; for he came head downwards, his helmet and his bayonet stuck in between the flagstones, and his one leg up in the air. The servant maid and the little boy went down stairs directly to look for him; but he was nowhere to be seen, although once they nearly trod upon him. If he had called out, 'Here I am,' it would have been all right, but he was too proud to cry out for help while he wore a uniform.

Presently it began to rain, and the drops fell faster and faster, till there was a heavy shower. When it was over, two boys happened to pass by, and one of them said, 'Look, there is a tin soldier. He ought to have a boat to sail in.'

So they made a boat out of a newspaper, and placed the tin soldier in it, and sent him sailing down the gutter, while the two boys ran by the side of it, and clapped their hands. Good gracious, what large waves arose in that gutter! and how fast the stream rolled on! for the rain had been very heavy. The paper boat rocked up and down, and turned itself round sometimes so quickly that the tin soldier trembled; yet he remained firm; his countenance did not change; he looked straight before him, and shouldered his musket. Suddenly the boat shot under a bridge which formed a part of a drain, and then it was as dark as the tin soldier's box.

'Where am I going now?' thought he. 'This is the black goblin's fault, I am sure. Ah, well, if the little lady were only here with me in the boat, I should not care for any darkness.'

Suddenly there appeared a great water-rat, who lived in the drain.

'Have you a passport?' asked the rat, 'give it to me at once.' But the tin soldier remained silent and held his musket tighter than ever. The boat sailed on and the rat followed it. How he did gnash his teeth and cry out to the bits of wood and straw, 'Stop him, stop him; he has not paid toll, and has not shown his pass.' But the stream rushed on stronger and stronger. The tin soldier could already see daylight shining where the arch ended. Then he heard a roaring sound quite terrible enough to frighten the bravest man. At the end of the tunnel the drain fell into a large canal over a steep place, which made it as dangerous for him as a waterfall would be to us. He was too close to it to stop, so the boat rushed on, and the poor tin soldier could only hold himself as stiffly as possible, without moving an eyelid, to show that he was not afraid. The boat whirled round three or four times, and then filled with water to the very edge; nothing could save it from sinking. He now stood up to his neck in water, while deeper and deeper sank the boat, and the paper became soft and loose with the wet, till at last the water closed over the soldier's head. He thought of the elegant little dancer whom he should never see again, and the words of the song sounded in his ears—

'Farewell, warrior! ever brave, Drifting onward to thy grave.'

Then the paper boat fell to pieces, and the soldier sank into the water and immediately afterwards was swallowed up by a great fish. Oh how dark it was inside the fish! A great deal darker than in the tunnel, and narrower too, but the tin soldier continued firm, and lay at full length shouldering his musket. The fish swam to and fro, making the most wonderful movements, but at last he became quite still. After a while, a flash of lightning seemed to pass through him, and then the daylight approached, and a voice cried out, 'I declare here is the tin soldier.' The fish had been caught, taken to the market and sold to the cook, who took him into the kitchen and cut him open with a large knife. She picked up the soldier and held him by the waist between her finger and thumb, and carried him into the room. They were all anxious to see this wonderful soldier who had travelled about inside a fish; but he was not at all proud. They placed him on the table, and—how many curious things do happen in the world!—there he was in the very same room from the window of which he had fallen, there were the same children, the same playthings, standing on the table, and the pretty castle with the elegant little dancer at the door; she still balanced herself on one leg, and held up the other, so she was as firm as himself.

It touched the tin soldier so much to see her that he almost wept tin tears, but he kept them back. He only looked at her and they both remained silent. Presently one of the little boys took up the tin soldier, and threw him into the stove. He had no reason for doing so, therefore it must have been the fault of the black goblin who lived in the snuff-box. The flames lighted up the tin soldier, as he stood, the heat was very terrible, but whether it proceeded from the real fire or from the fire of love he could not tell. Then he could see that the bright colors were faded from his uniform, but whether they had been washed off during his journey or from the effects of his sorrow, no one could say. He looked at the little lady, and she looked at him. He felt himself melting away, but he still remained firm with his gun on his shoulder. Suddenly the door of the room flew open and the draught of air caught up the little dancer, she fluttered like a sylph right into the stove by the side of the tin soldier, and was instantly in flames and was gone. The tin soldier melted down into a lump, and the next morning, when the maid servant took the ashes out of the stove, she found him in the shape of a little tin heart. But of the little dancer nothing remained but the tinsel rose, which was burnt black as a cinder.

LITTLE RED RIDING HOOD

Brothers Grimm

Once upon a time there was a dear little girl who was loved by everyone who looked at her, but most of all by her grandmother, and there was nothing that she would not have given to the child. Once she gave her a little cap of red velvet, which suited her so well that she would never wear anything else; so she was always called 'Little Red-Cap.'

One day her mother said to her: 'Come, Little Red-Cap, here is a piece of cake and a bottle of wine; take them to your grandmother, she is ill and weak, and they will do her good. Set out before it gets hot, and when you are going, walk nicely and quietly and do not run off the path, or you may fall and break the bottle, and then your grandmother will get nothing; and when you go into her room, don't forget to say, 'Good morning', and don't peep into every corner before you do it.'

'I will take great care,' said Little Red-Cap to her mother, and gave her hand on it.

The grandmother lived out in the wood, half a league from the village, and just as Little Red-Cap entered the wood, a wolf met her. Red-Cap did not know what a wicked creature he was, and was not at all afraid of him.

'Good day, Little Red-Cap,' said he.

'Thank you kindly, wolf.'

'Whither away so early, Little Red-Cap?'

'To my grandmother's.'

'What have you got in your apron?'

'Cake and wine; yesterday was baking-day, so poor sick grandmother is to have something good, to make her stronger.'

'Where does your grandmother live, Little Red-Cap?'

'A good quarter of a league farther on in the wood; her house stands under the three large oak-trees, the nut-trees are just below; you surely must know it,' replied Little Red-Cap.

The wolf thought to himself: 'What a tender young creature! what a nice plump mouthful—she will be better to eat than the old woman. I must act craftily, so as to catch both.' So he walked for a short time by the side of Little Red-Cap, and then he said: 'See, Little Red-Cap, how pretty the flowers are about here—why do you not look round? I believe, too, that you do not hear how sweetly the little birds are singing; you walk gravely along as if you were going to school, while everything else out here in the wood is merry.'

Little Red-Cap raised her eyes, and when she saw the sunbeams dancing here and there through the trees, and pretty flowers growing everywhere, she thought: 'Suppose I take grandmother a fresh nosegay; that would please her too. It is so early in the day that I shall still get there in good time'; and so she ran from the path into the wood to look for flowers. And whenever she had picked one, she fancied that she saw a still prettier one farther on, and ran after it, and so got deeper and deeper into the wood.

Meanwhile the wolf ran straight to the grandmother's house and knocked at the door.

'Who is there?'

'Little Red-Cap,' replied the wolf. 'She is bringing cake and wine; open the door.'

'Lift the latch,' called out the grandmother, 'I am too weak, and cannot get up.'

The wolf lifted the latch, the door sprang open, and without saying a word he went straight to the grandmother's bed, and devoured her. Then he put on her clothes, dressed himself in her cap laid himself in bed and drew the curtains.

Little Red-Cap, however, had been running about picking flowers, and when she had gathered so many that she could carry no more, she remembered her grandmother, and set out on the way to her.

She was surprised to find the cottage-door standing open, and when she went into the room, she had such a strange feeling that she said to herself: 'Oh dear! how uneasy I feel today, and at other times I like being with grandmother so much.' She called out: 'Good morning,' but received no answer; so she went to the bed and drew back the curtains. There lay her grandmother with her cap pulled far over her face, and looking very strange.

'Oh! grandmother,' she said, 'what big ears you have!'

'The better to hear you with, my child,' was the reply.

'But, grandmother, what big eyes you have!' she said.

'The better to see you with, my dear.'

'But, grandmother, what large hands you have!'

'The better to hug you with.'

'Oh! but, grandmother, what a terrible big mouth you have!'

'The better to eat you with!'

And scarcely had the wolf said this, than with one bound he was out of bed and swallowed up Red-Cap.

When the wolf had appeased his appetite, he lay down again in the bed, fell asleep and began to snore very loud. The huntsman was just passing the house, and thought to himself: 'How the old woman is snoring! I must just see if she wants anything.' So he went into the room, and when he came to the bed, he saw that the wolf was lying in it. 'Do I find you here, you old sinner!' said he. 'I have long sought you!' Then just as he was going to fire at him, it occurred to him that the wolf might have devoured the grandmother, and that she might still be saved, so he did not fire, but took a pair of scissors, and began to cut open the stomach of the sleeping wolf. When he had made two snips, he saw the little Red-

Cap shining, and then he made two snips more, and the little girl sprang out, crying: 'Ah, how frightened I have been! How dark it was inside the wolf'; and after that the aged grandmother came out alive also, but scarcely able to breathe. Red-Cap, however, quickly fetched great stones with which they filled the wolf's belly, and when he awoke, he wanted to run away, but the stones were so heavy that he collapsed at once, and fell dead.

Then all three were delighted. The huntsman drew off the wolf's skin and went home with it; the grandmother ate the cake and drank the wine which Red-Cap had brought, and revived, but Red-Cap thought to herself: 'As long as I live, I will never by myself leave the path, to run into the wood, when my mother has forbidden me to do so.'

It also related that once when Red-Cap was again taking cakes to the old grandmother, another wolf spoke to her, and tried to entice her from the path. Red-Cap, however, was on her guard, and went straight forward on her way, and told her grandmother that she had met the wolf, and that he had said 'good morning' to her, but with such a wicked look in his eyes, that if they had not been on the public road she was certain he would have eaten her up. 'Well,' said the grandmother, 'we will shut the door, that he may not come in.' Soon afterwards the wolf knocked, and cried: 'Open the door, grandmother, I am Little Red-Cap, and am bringing you some cakes.' But they did not speak, or open the door, so the grey-beard stole twice or thrice round the house, and at last jumped on the roof, intending to wait until Red-Cap went home in the evening, and then to steal after her and devour her in the darkness. But the grandmother saw what was in his thoughts. In front of the house was a great stone trough, so she said to the child: 'Take the pail, Red-Cap; I made some sausages yesterday, so carry the water in which I boiled them to the trough.' Red-Cap carried until the great trough was quite full. Then the smell of the sausages reached the wolf, and he sniffed and peeped down, and at last stretched out his neck so far that he could no longer keep his footing and began to slip, and slipped down from the roof straight into the great trough, and was drowned. But Red-Cap went joyously home, and no one ever did anything to harm her again.

RUMPELSTILTSKIN

Brothers Grimm

By the side of a wood, in a country a long way off, ran a fine stream of water; and upon the stream there stood a mill. The miller's house was close by, and the miller, you must know, had a very beautiful daughter. She was, moreover, very shrewd and clever; and the miller was so proud of her, that he one day told the king of the land, who used to come and hunt in the wood, that his daughter could spin gold out of straw. Now this king was very fond of money; and when he heard the miller's boast his greediness was raised, and he sent for the girl to be brought before him. Then he led her to a chamber in his palace where there was a great heap of straw, and gave her a spinning-wheel, and said, 'All this must be spun into gold before morning, as you love your life.' It was in vain that the poor maiden said that it was only a silly boast of her father, for that she could do no such thing as spin straw into gold: the chamber door was locked, and she was left alone.

She sat down in one corner of the room, and began to bewail her hard fate; when on a sudden the door opened, and a droll-looking little man hobbled in, and said, 'Good morrow to you, my good lass; what are you weeping for?' 'Alas!' said she, 'I must spin this straw into gold, and I know not how.' 'What will you give me,' said the hobgoblin, 'to do it for you?' 'My necklace,' replied the maiden. He took her at her word, and sat himself down to the wheel, and whistled and sang:

Round about, round about,
Lo and behold!
Reel away, reel away,
Straw into gold!

And round about the wheel went merrily; the work was quickly done, and the straw was all spun into gold.

When the king came and saw this, he was greatly astonished and pleased; but his heart grew still more greedy of gain, and he shut up the poor miller's daughter again with a fresh task. Then she knew not what to do, and sat down once more to weep; but the dwarf soon opened the door, and said, 'What will you give me to do your task?' 'The ring on my finger,' said she. So her little friend took the ring, and began to work at the wheel again, and whistled and sang:

Round about, round about,

Lo and behold!
Reel away, reel away,
Straw into gold!
Till, long before morning, all was done again.

The king was greatly delighted to see all this glittering treasure; but still he had not enough: so he took the miller's daughter to a yet larger heap, and said, 'All this must be spun tonight; and if it is, you shall be my queen.' As soon as she was alone that dwarf came in, and said, 'What will you give me to spin gold for you this third time?' 'I have nothing left,' said she. 'Then say you will give me,' said the little man, 'the first little child that you may have when you are queen.' 'That may never be,' thought the miller's daughter: and as she knew no other way to get her task done, she said she would do what he asked. Round went the wheel again to the old song, and the manikin once more spun the heap into gold. The king came in the morning, and, finding all he wanted, was forced to keep his word; so he married the miller's daughter, and she really became queen.

At the birth of her first little child she was very glad, and forgot the dwarf, and what she had said. But one day he came into her room, where she was sitting playing with her baby, and put her in mind of it. Then she grieved sorely at her misfortune, and said she would give him all the wealth of the kingdom if he would let her off, but in vain; till at last her tears softened him, and he said, 'I will give you three days' grace, and if during that time you tell me my name, you shall keep your child.'

Now the queen lay awake all night, thinking of all the odd names that she had ever heard; and she sent messengers all over the land to find out new ones. The next day the little man came, and she began with TIMOTHY, ICHABOD, BENJAMIN, JEREMIAH, and all the names she could remember; but to all and each of them he said, 'Madam, that is not my name.'

The second day she began with all the comical names she could hear of, BANDY-LEGS, HUNCHBACK, CROOK-SHANKS, and so on; but the little gentleman still said to every one of them, 'Madam, that is not my name.'

The third day one of the messengers came back, and said, 'I have travelled two days without hearing of any other names; but yesterday, as I was climbing a high hill, among the trees of the forest where the fox and the hare bid each other good night, I saw a little hut; and before the hut burnt a fire; and round about the fire a funny little dwarf was dancing upon one leg, and singing:

Merrily the feast I'll make.
Today I'll brew, tomorrow bake;
Merrily I'll dance and sing,
For next day will a stranger bring.
Little does my lady dream
Rumpelstiltskin is my name!

When the queen heard this she jumped for joy, and as soon as her little friend came she sat down upon her throne, and called all her court round to enjoy the fun; and the nurse stood by her side with the baby in her arms, as if it was quite ready to be given up. Then the little man began to chuckle at the thought of having the poor child, to take home with him to his hut in the woods; and he cried out, 'Now, lady, what is my name?' 'Is it JOHN?' asked she. 'No, madam!' 'Is it TOM?' 'No, madam!' 'Is it JEMMY?' 'It is not.' 'Can your name be RUMPELSTILTSKIN?' said the lady slyly. 'Some witch told you that!—some witch told you that!' cried the little man, and dashed his right foot in a rage so deep into the floor, that he was forced to lay hold of it with both hands to pull it out.

Then he made the best of his way off, while the nurse laughed and the baby crowed; and all the court jeered at him for having had so much trouble for nothing, and said, 'We wish you a very good morning, and a merry feast, Mr RUMPLESTILTSKIN!'

THE JUNIPER TREE

Brothers Grimm

Long, long ago, some two thousand years or so, there lived a rich man with a good and beautiful wife. They loved each other dearly, but sorrowed much that they had no children. So greatly did they desire to have one, that the wife prayed for it day and night, but still they remained childless.

In front of the house there was a court, in which grew a juniper-tree. One winter's day the wife stood under the tree to peel some apples, and as she was peeling them, she cut her finger, and the blood fell on the snow. 'Ah,' sighed the woman heavily, 'if I had but a child, as red as blood and as white as snow,' and as she spoke the words, her heart grew light within her, and it seemed to her that her wish was granted, and she returned to the house feeling glad and comforted. A month passed, and the snow had all disappeared; then another month went by, and all the earth was green. So the months followed one another, and first the trees budded in the woods, and soon the green branches grew thickly intertwined, and then the blossoms began to fall. Once again the wife stood under the juniper-tree, and it was so full of sweet scent that her heart leaped for joy, and she was so overcome with her happiness, that she fell on her knees. Presently the fruit became round and firm, and she was glad and at peace; but when they were fully ripe she picked the berries and ate eagerly of them, and then she grew sad and ill. A little while later she called her husband, and said to him, weeping. 'If I die, bury me under the juniper-tree.' Then she felt comforted and happy again, and before another month had passed she had a little child, and when she saw that it was as white as snow and as red as blood, her joy was so great that she died.

Her husband buried her under the juniper-tree, and wept bitterly for her. By degrees, however, his sorrow grew less, and although at times he still grieved over his loss, he was able to go about as usual, and later on he married again.

He now had a little daughter born to him; the child of his first wife was a boy, who was as red as blood and as white as snow. The mother loved her daughter very much, and when she looked at her and then looked at the boy, it pierced her heart to think that he would always stand in the way of her own child, and she was continually thinking how she could get the whole of the property for her. This evil thought took possession of her more and more, and made her behave very unkindly to the boy. She drove him from place to place with cuffings and buffetings, so that the poor child went about in fear, and had no peace from the time he left school to the time he went back.

One day the little daughter came running to her mother in the store-room, and said, 'Mother, give me an apple.' 'Yes, my child,' said the wife, and she gave her a beautiful apple out of the chest; the chest had a very heavy lid and a large iron lock.

'Mother,' said the little daughter again, 'may not brother have one too?' The mother was angry at this, but she answered, 'Yes, when he comes out of school.'

Just then she looked out of the window and saw him coming, and it seemed as if an evil spirit entered into her, for she snatched the apple out of her little daughter's hand, and said, 'You shall not have one before your brother.' She threw the apple into the chest and shut it to. The little boy now came in, and the evil spirit in the wife made her say kindly to him, 'My son, will you have an apple?' but she gave him a wicked look. 'Mother,' said the boy, 'how dreadful you look! Yes, give me an apple.' The thought came to her that she would kill him. 'Come with me,' she said, and she lifted up the lid of the chest; 'take one out for yourself.' And as he bent over to do so, the evil spirit urged her, and crash! down went the lid, and off went the little boy's head. Then she was overwhelmed with fear at the thought of what she had done. 'If only I can prevent anyone knowing that I did it,' she thought. So she went upstairs to her room, and took a white handkerchief out of her top drawer; then she set the boy's head again on his shoulders, and bound it with the handkerchief so that nothing could be seen, and placed him on a chair by the door with an apple in his hand.

Soon after this, little Marleen came up to her mother who was stirring a pot of boiling water over the fire, and said, 'Mother, brother is sitting by the door with an apple in his hand, and he looks so pale; and when I asked him to give me the apple, he did not answer, and that frightened me.'

'Go to him again,' said her mother, 'and if he does not answer, give him a box on the ear.' So little Marleen went, and said, 'Brother, give me that apple,' but he did not say a word; then she gave him a box on the ear, and his head rolled off. She was so terrified at this, that she ran crying and screaming to her mother. 'Oh!' she said, 'I have knocked off brother's head,' and then she wept and wept, and nothing would stop her.

'What have you done!' said her mother, 'but no one must know about it, so you must keep silence; what is done can't be undone; we will make him into puddings.' And she took the little boy and cut him up, made him into puddings, and put him in the pot. But Marleen stood looking on, and wept and wept, and her tears fell into the pot, so that there was no need of salt.

Presently the father came home and sat down to his dinner; he asked, 'Where is my son?' The mother said nothing, but gave him a large dish of black pudding, and Marleen still wept without ceasing.

The father again asked, 'Where is my son?'

'Oh,' answered the wife, 'he is gone into the country to his mother's great uncle; he is going to stay there some time.'

'What has he gone there for, and he never even said goodbye to me!'

'Well, he likes being there, and he told me he should be away quite six weeks; he is well looked after there.'

'I feel very unhappy about it,' said the husband, 'in case it should not be all right, and he ought to have said goodbye to me.'

With this he went on with his dinner, and said, 'Little Marleen, why do you weep? Brother will soon be back.' Then he asked his wife for more pudding, and as he ate, he threw the bones under the table.

Little Marleen went upstairs and took her best silk handkerchief out of her bottom drawer, and in it she wrapped all the bones from under the table and carried them outside, and all the time she did nothing but weep. Then she laid them in the green grass under the juniper-tree, and she had no sooner done so, then all her sadness seemed to leave her, and she wept no more. And now the juniper-tree began to move, and the branches waved backwards and forwards, first away from one another, and then together again, as it might be someone clapping their hands for joy. After this a mist came round the tree, and in the midst of it there was a burning as of fire, and out of the fire there flew a beautiful bird, that rose high into the air, singing magnificently, and when it could no more be seen, the juniper-tree stood there as before, and the silk handkerchief and the bones were gone.

Little Marleen now felt as lighthearted and happy as if her brother were still alive, and she went back to the house and sat down cheerfully to the table and ate.

The bird flew away and alighted on the house of a goldsmith and began to sing:

My mother killed her little son;
My father grieved when I was gone;
My sister loved me best of all;
She laid her kerchief over me,
And took my bones that they might lie
Underneath the juniper-tree
Kywitt, Kywitt, what a beautiful bird am I!

The goldsmith was in his workshop making a gold chain, when he heard the song of the bird on his roof. He thought it so beautiful that he got up and ran out, and as he crossed the threshold he lost one of his slippers. But he ran on into the middle of the street, with a slipper on one foot and a sock on the other; he still had on his apron, and still held the gold chain and the pincers in his hands, and so he stood gazing up at the bird, while the sun came shining brightly down on the street.

'Bird,' he said, 'how beautifully you sing! Sing me that song again.'

'Nay,' said the bird, 'I do not sing twice for nothing.

Give that gold chain, and I will sing it you again.'

'Here is the chain, take it,' said the goldsmith. 'Only sing me that again.'

The bird flew down and took the gold chain in his right claw, and then he alighted again in front of the goldsmith and sang:

My mother killed her little son;
My father grieved when I was gone;
My sister loved me best of all;
She laid her kerchief over me,
And took my bones that they might lie
Underneath the juniper-tree
Kywitt, Kywitt, what a beautiful bird am I!

Then he flew away, and settled on the roof of a shoemaker's house and sang:

My mother killed her little son;
My father grieved when I was gone;
My sister loved me best of all;
She laid her kerchief over me,
And took my bones that they might lie
Underneath the juniper-tree
Kywitt, Kywitt, what a beautiful bird am I!

The shoemaker heard him, and he jumped up and ran out in his shirt-sleeves, and stood looking up at the bird on the roof with his hand over his eyes to keep himself from being blinded by the sun.

'Bird,' he said, 'how beautifully you sing!' Then he

called through the door to his wife: 'Wife, come out; here is a bird, come and look at it and hear how beautifully it sings.' Then he called his daughter and the children, then the apprentices, girls and boys, and they all ran up the street to look at the bird, and saw how splendid it was with its red and green feathers, and its neck like burnished gold, and eyes like two bright stars in its head.

'Bird,' said the shoemaker, 'sing me that song again.'

'Nay,' answered the bird, 'I do not sing twice for nothing; you must give me something.'

'Wife,' said the man, 'go into the garret; on the upper shelf you will see a pair of red shoes; bring them to me.' The wife went in and fetched the shoes.

'There, bird,' said the shoemaker, 'now sing me that song again.'

The bird flew down and took the red shoes in his left claw, and then he went back to the roof and sang:

My mother killed her little son;
My father grieved when I was gone;
My sister loved me best of all;
She laid her kerchief over me,
And took my bones that they might lie
Underneath the juniper-tree
Kywitt, Kywitt, what a beautiful bird am I!

When he had finished, he flew away. He had the chain in his right claw and the shoes in his left, and he flew right away to a mill, and the mill went 'Click clack, click clack, click clack.' Inside the mill were twenty of the miller's men hewing a stone, and as they went 'Hick hack, hick hack, hick hack,' the mill went 'Click clack, click clack, click clack.'

The bird settled on a lime-tree in front of the mill and sang:

My mother killed her little son;
then one of the men left off,
My father grieved when I was gone;
two more men left off and listened,
My sister loved me best of all;
then four more left off,
She laid her kerchief over me,
And took my bones that they might lie
Now there were only eight at work,
Underneath,
and now only five,
the juniper-tree.
and now only one,
Kywitt, Kywitt, what a beautiful bird am I!

then he looked up and the last one had left off work.

'Bird,' he said, 'what a beautiful song that is you sing! Let me hear it too; sing it again.'

'Nay,' answered the bird, 'I do not sing twice for nothing; give me that millstone, and I will sing it again.'

'If it belonged to me alone,' said the man, 'you should have it.'

'Yes, yes,' said the others: 'if he will sing again, he can have it.'

The bird came down, and all the twenty millers set to and lifted up the stone with a beam; then the bird put his head through the hole and took the stone round his neck like a collar, and flew back with it to the tree and sang—

My mother killed her little son;
My father grieved when I was gone;
My sister loved me best of all;
She laid her kerchief over me,
And took my bones that they might lie
Underneath the juniper-tree
Kywitt, Kywitt, what a beautiful bird am I!

And when he had finished his song, he spread his wings, and with the chain in his right claw, the shoes in his left, and the millstone round his neck, he flew right away to his father's house.

The father, the mother, and little Marleen were having their dinner.

'How lighthearted I feel,' said the father, 'so pleased and cheerful.'

'And I,' said the mother, 'I feel so uneasy, as if a heavy thunderstorm were coming.'

But little Marleen sat and wept and wept.

Then the bird came flying towards the house and settled on the roof.

'I do feel so happy,' said the father, 'and how beautifully the sun shines; I feel just as if I were going to see an old friend again.'

'Ah!' said the wife, 'and I am so full of distress and

uneasiness that my teeth chatter, and I feel as if there were a fire in my veins,' and she tore open her dress; and all the while little Marleen sat in the corner and wept, and the plate on her knees was wet with her tears.

The bird now flew to the juniper-tree and began singing:

'My mother killed her little son;

the mother shut her eyes and her ears, that she might see and hear nothing, but there was a roaring sound in her ears like that of a violent storm, and in her eyes a burning and flashing like lightning:

My father grieved when I was gone;

'Look, mother,' said the man, 'at the beautiful bird that is singing so magnificently; and how warm and bright the sun is, and what a delicious scent of spice in the air!'

My sister loved me best of all;

then little Marleen laid her head down on her knees and sobbed.

'I must go outside and see the bird nearer,' said the man.

'Ah, do not go!' cried the wife. 'I feel as if the whole house were in flames!'

But the man went out and looked at the bird.
She laid her kerchief over me,
And took my bones that they might lie
Underneath the juniper-tree
Kywitt, Kywitt, what a beautiful bird am I!'

With that the bird let fall the gold chain, and it fell just round the man's neck, so that it fitted him exactly.

He went inside, and said, 'See, what a splendid bird

that is; he has given me this beautiful gold chain, and looks so beautiful himself.'

But the wife was in such fear and trouble, that she fell on the floor, and her cap fell from her head.

Then the bird began again:

My mother killed her little son;
Ah me! cried the wife, 'if I were but a thousand feet
beneath the earth, that I might not hear that song.
My father grieved when I was gone;
then the woman fell down again as if dead.
My sister loved me best of all

'Well,' said little Marleen, 'I will go out too and see if the bird will give me anything.'

So she went out.
She laid her kerchief over me,
And took my bones that they might lie
and he threw down the shoes to her,
Underneath the juniper-tree
Kywitt, Kywitt, what a beautiful bird am I!

And she now felt quite happy and lighthearted; she put on the shoes and danced and jumped about in them. 'I was so miserable,' she said, 'when I came out, but that has all passed away; that is indeed a splendid bird, and he has given me a pair of red shoes.'

The wife sprang up, with her hair standing out from her head like flames of fire. 'Then I will go out too,' she said, 'and see if it will lighten my misery, for I feel as if the world were coming to an end.'

But as she crossed the threshold, crash! the bird threw the millstone down on her head, and she was crushed to death.

The father and little Marleen heard the sound and ran out, but they only saw mist and flame and fire rising from the spot, and when these had passed, there stood the little brother, and he took the father and little Marleen by the hand; then they all three rejoiced, and went inside together and sat down to their dinners and ate.

THE GOOSE-GIRL

Brothers Grimm

The king of a great land died, and left his queen to take care of their only child. This child was a daughter, who was very beautiful; and her mother loved her dearly, and was very kind to her. And there was a good fairy too, who was fond of the princess, and helped her mother to watch over her. When she grew up, she was betrothed to a prince who lived a great way off; and as the time drew near for her to be married, she got ready to set off on her journey to his country. Then the queen her mother, packed up a great many costly things; jewels, and gold, and silver; trinkets, fine dresses, and in short everything that became a royal bride. And she gave her a waiting-maid to ride with her, and give her into the bridegroom's hands; and each had a horse for the journey. Now the princess's horse was the fairy's gift, and it was called

Falada, and could speak.

When the time came for them to set out, the fairy went into her bed-chamber, and took a little knife, and cut off a lock of her hair, and gave it to the princess, and said, 'Take care of it, dear child; for it is a charm that may be of use to you on the road.' Then they all took a sorrowful leave of the princess; and she put the lock of hair into her bosom, got upon her horse, and set off on her journey to her bridegroom's kingdom.

One day, as they were riding along by a brook, the princess began to feel very thirsty: and she said to her maid, 'Pray get down, and fetch me some water in my golden cup out of yonder brook, for I want to drink.' 'Nay,' said the maid, 'if you are thirsty, get off yourself, and stoop down by the water and drink; I shall not be your waiting-maid any longer.' Then she was so thirsty that she got down, and knelt over the little brook, and drank; for she was frightened, and dared not bring out her golden cup; and she wept and said, 'Alas! what will become of me?' And the lock answered her, and said:

'Alas! alas! if thy mother knew it,
Sadly, sadly, would she rue it.'

But the princess was very gentle and meek, so she said nothing to her maid's ill behaviour, but got upon her horse again.

Then all rode farther on their journey, till the day grew so warm, and the sun so scorching, that the bride began to feel very thirsty again; and at last, when they came to a river, she forgot her maid's rude speech, and said, 'Pray get down, and fetch me some water to drink in my golden cup.' But the maid answered her, and even spoke more haughtily than before: 'Drink if you will, but I shall not be your waiting-maid.' Then the princess was so thirsty that she got off her horse, and lay down, and held her head over the running stream, and cried and said, 'What will become of me?' And the lock of hair answered her again:

Alas! alas! if thy mother knew it,
Sadly, sadly, would she rue it.

And as she leaned down to drink, the lock of hair fell from her bosom, and floated away with the water. Now she was so frightened that she did not see it; but her maid saw it, and was very glad, for she knew the charm; and she saw that the poor bride would be in her power, now that she had lost the hair. So when the bride had done drinking, and would have got upon Falada again, the maid said, 'I shall ride upon Falada, and you may have my horse instead'; so she was forced to give up her horse, and soon afterwards to take off her royal clothes and put on her maid's shabby ones.

At last, as they drew near the end of their journey, this treacherous servant threatened to kill her mistress if she ever told anyone what had happened. But Falada saw it all, and marked it well.

Then the waiting-maid got upon Falada, and the real bride rode upon the other horse, and they went on in this way till at last they came to the royal court. There was great joy at their coming, and the prince flew to meet them, and lifted the maid from her horse, thinking she was the one who was to be his wife; and she was led upstairs to the royal chamber; but the true princess was told to stay in the court below.

Now the old king happened just then to have nothing else to do; so he amused himself by sitting at his kitchen window, looking at what was going on; and he saw her in the courtyard. As she looked very pretty, and too delicate for a waiting-maid, he went up into the royal chamber to ask the bride who it was she had brought with her, that was thus left standing in the court below. 'I brought her with me for the sake of her company on the road,' said she; 'pray give the girl some work to do, that she may not be idle.' The old king could not for some time think of any work for her to do; but at last he said, 'I have a lad who takes care of my geese; she may go and help him.' Now the name of this lad, that the real bride was to help in watching the king's geese, was Curdken.

But the false bride said to the prince, 'Dear husband, pray do me one piece of kindness.' 'That I will,' said the prince. 'Then tell one of your slaughterers to cut off the head of the horse I rode upon, for it was very unruly, and plagued me sadly on the road'; but the truth was, she was very much afraid lest Falada should some day or other speak, and tell all she had done to the princess. She carried her point, and the faithful Falada was killed; but when the true princess heard of it, she wept, and begged the man to nail up Falada's head against a large dark gate of the city, through which she had to pass every morning and evening, that there she might still see him sometimes. Then the slaughterer said he would do as she wished; and cut off the head, and nailed it up under the dark gate.

Early the next morning, as she and Curdken went out through the gate, she said sorrowfully:

'Falada, Falada, there thou hangest!' and the head answered:

Bride, bride, there thou gangest!
Alas! alas! if thy mother knew it,
Sadly, sadly, would she rue it.

Then they went out of the city, and drove the geese on. And when she came to the meadow, she sat down upon a bank there, and let down her waving locks of hair, which were all of pure silver; and when Curdken saw it glitter in the sun, he ran up, and would have pulled some of the locks out, but she cried:

Blow, breezes, blow!
Let Curdken's hat go!
Blow, breezes, blow!
Let him after it go!
O'er hills, dales, and rocks,
Away be it whirl'd
Till the silvery locks
Are all comb'd and curl'd!

Then there came a wind, so strong that it blew off

Curdken's hat; and away it flew over the hills: and he was forced to turn and run after it; till, by the time he came back, she had done combing and curling her hair, and had put it up again safe. Then he was very angry and sulky, and would not speak to her at all; but they watched the geese until it grew dark in the evening, and then drove them homewards.

The next morning, as they were going through the dark gate, the poor girl looked up at Falada's head, and cried:

'Falada, Falada, there thou hangest!' and the head answered:

Bride, bride, there thou gangest!
Alas! alas! if thy mother knew it,
Sadly, sadly, would she rue it.

Then she drove on the geese, and sat down again in the meadow, and began to comb out her hair as before; and Curdken ran up to her, and wanted to take hold of it; but she cried out quickly:

Blow, breezes, blow!
Let Curdken's hat go!
Blow, breezes, blow!
Let him after it go!
O'er hills, dales, and rocks,
Away be it whirl'd
Till the silvery locks
Are all comb'd and curl'd!

Then the wind came and blew away his hat; and off it

flew a great way, over the hills and far away, so that he had to run after it; and when he came back she had bound up her hair again, and all was safe. So they watched the geese till it grew dark.

In the evening, after they came home, Curdken went to the old king, and said, 'I cannot have that strange girl to help me to keep the geese any longer.' 'Why?' said the king. 'Because, instead of doing any good, she does nothing but tease me all day long.' Then the king made him tell him what had happened. And Curdken said, 'When we go in the morning through the dark gate with our flock of geese, she cries and talks with the head of a horse that hangs upon the wall, and says:

'Falada, Falada, there thou hangest!' and the head answers:

Bride, bride, there thou gangest!
Alas! alas! if thy mother knew it,
Sadly, sadly, would she rue it.

And Curdken went on telling the king what had happened upon the meadow where the geese fed; how his hat was blown away; and how he was forced to run after it, and to leave his flock of geese to themselves. But the old king told the boy to go out again the next day: and when morning came, he placed himself behind the dark gate, and heard how she spoke to Falada, and how Falada answered. Then he went into the field, and hid himself in a bush by the meadow's side; and he soon saw with his own eyes how they drove the flock of geese; and how, after a little time, she let down her hair that glittered in the sun. And then he heard her say:

Blow, breezes, blow!
Let Curdken's hat go!
Blow, breezes, blow!
Let him after it go!
O'er hills, dales, and rocks,
Away be it whirl'd
Till the silvery locks
Are all comb'd and curl'd!

And soon came a gale of wind, and carried away Curdken's hat, and away went Curdken after it, while the girl went on combing and curling her hair. All this the old king saw: so he went home without being seen; and when the little goose-girl came back in the evening he called her aside, and asked her why she did so: but she burst into tears, and said, 'That I must not tell you or any man, or I shall lose my life.'

But the old king begged so hard, that she had no peace till she had told him all the tale, from beginning to end, word for word. And it was very lucky for her that she did so, for when she had done the king ordered royal clothes to be put upon her, and gazed on her with wonder, she was so beautiful. Then he called his son and told him that he had only a false bride; for that she was merely a waiting-maid, while the true bride stood by. And the young king rejoiced when he saw her beauty, and heard how meek and patient she had been; and without saying anything to the false bride, the king ordered a great feast to be got ready for all his court. The bridegroom sat at the top, with the false princess on one side, and the true one on the other; but nobody knew her again, for her beauty was quite dazzling to their eyes; and she did not seem at all like the little goose-girl, now that she had her brilliant dress on.

When they had eaten and drank, and were very merry, the old king said he would tell them a tale. So he began, and told all the story of the princess, as if it was one that he had once heard; and he asked the true waiting-maid what she thought ought to be done to anyone who would behave thus. 'Nothing better,' said this false bride, 'than that she should be thrown into a cask stuck round with sharp nails, and that two white horses should be put to it, and should drag it from street to street till she was dead.' 'Thou art she!' said the old king; 'and as thou has judged thyself, so shall it be done to thee.' And the young king was then married to his true wife, and they reigned over the kingdom in peace and happiness all their lives; and the good fairy came to see them, and restored the faithful Falada to life again.

THE DRYAD

Hans Christian Andersen

We are travelling to Paris to the Exhibition.

Now we are there. That was a journey, a flight without magic. We flew on the wings of steam over the sea and across the land.

Yes, our time is the time of fairy tales.

We are in the midst of Paris, in a great hotel. Blooming flowers ornament the staircases, and soft carpets the floors.

Our room is a very cosy one, and through the open balcony door we have a view of a great square. Spring lives down there; it has come to Paris, and arrived at the same time with us. It has come in the shape of a glorious young chestnut tree, with delicate leaves newly opened. How the tree gleams, dressed in its spring garb, before all the other trees in the place! One of these latter had been struck out of the list of living trees. It lies on the ground with roots exposed. On the place where it stood, the young chestnut tree is to be planted, and to flourish.

It still stands towering aloft on the heavy wagon which has brought it this morning a distance of several miles to Paris. For years it had stood there, in the protection of a mighty oak tree, under which the old venerable clergyman had often sat, with children listening to his stories.

The young chestnut tree had also listened to the stories; for the Dryad who lived in it was a child also. She remembered the time when the tree was so little that it only projected a short way above the grass and ferns around. These were as tall as they would ever be; but the tree grew every year, and enjoyed the air and the sunshine, and drank the dew and the rain. Several times it was also, as it must be, well shaken by the wind and the rain; for that is a part of education.

The Dryad rejoiced in her life, and rejoiced in the sunshine, and the singing of the birds; but she was most rejoiced at human voices; she understood the language of men as well as she understood that of animals.

Butterflies, cockchafers, dragon-flies, everything that could fly came to pay a visit. They could all talk. They told of the village, of the vineyard, of the forest, of the old castle with its parks and canals and ponds. Down in the water dwelt also living beings, which, in their way, could fly under the water from one place to another—beings with knowledge and delineation. They said nothing at all; they were so clever!

And the swallow, who had dived, told about the

pretty little goldfish, of the thick turbot, the fat brill, and the old carp. The swallow could describe all that very well, but, 'Self is the man,' she said. 'One ought to see these things one's self.' But how was the Dryad ever to see such beings? She was obliged to be satisfied with being able to look over the beautiful country and see the busy industry of men.

It was glorious; but most glorious of all when the old clergyman sat under the oak tree and talked of France, and of the great deeds of her sons and daughters, whose names will be mentioned with admiration through all time.

Then the Dryad heard of the shepherd girl, Joan of Arc, and of Charlotte Corday; she heard about Henry the Fourth, and Napoleon the First; she heard names whose echo sounds in the hearts of the people.

The village children listened attentively, and the Dryad no less attentively; she became a school-child with the rest. In the clouds that went sailing by she saw, picture by picture, everything that she heard talked about. The cloudy sky was her picture-book.

She felt so happy in beautiful France, the fruitful land of genius, with the crater of freedom. But in her heart the sting remained that the bird, that every animal that could fly, was much better off than she. Even the fly could look about more in the world, far beyond the Dryad's horizon.

France was so great and so glorious, but she could only look across a little piece of it. The land stretched out, world-wide, with vineyards, forests and great cities. Of all these Paris was the most splendid and the mightiest. The birds could get there; but she, never!

Among the village children was a little ragged, poor girl, but a pretty one to look at. She was always laughing or singing and twining red flowers in her black hair.

'Don't go to Paris!' the old clergyman warned her. 'Poor child! if you go there, it will be your ruin.'

But she went for all that.

The Dryad often thought of her; for she had the same wish, and felt the same longing for the great city.

The Dryad's tree was bearing its first chestnut blossoms; the birds were twittering round them in the most beautiful sunshine. Then a stately carriage came rolling along that way, and in it sat a grand lady driving the spirited, light-footed horses. On the back seat a little smart groom balanced himself. The Dryad knew the lady, and the old clergyman knew her also. He shook his head gravely when he saw her, and said:

'So you went there after all, and it was your ruin, poor Mary!'

'That one poor?' thought the Dryad. 'No; she wears a dress fit for a countess' (she had become one in the city of magic changes). 'Oh, if I were only there, amid all the splendor and pomp! They shine up into the very clouds at night; when I look up, I can tell in what direction the town lies.'

Towards that direction the Dryad looked every evening. She saw in the dark night the gleaming cloud on the horizon; in the clear moonlight nights she missed the sailing clouds, which showed her pictures of the city and pictures from history.

The child grasps at the picture-books, the Dryad grasped at the cloud-world, her thought-book. A sudden, cloudless sky was for her a blank leaf; and for several days she had only had such leaves before her.

It was in the warm summer-time: not a breeze moved through the glowing hot days. Every leaf, every flower, lay as if it were torpid, and the people seemed torpid, too.

Then the clouds arose and covered the region round about where the gleaming mist announced 'Here lies Paris.'

The clouds piled themselves up like a chain of mountains, hurried on through the air, and spread themselves abroad over the whole landscape, as far as the Dryad's eye could reach.

Like enormous blue-black blocks of rock, the clouds lay piled over one another. Gleams of lightning shot forth from them.

'These also are the servants of the Lord God,' the old clergyman had said. And there came a bluish dazzling flash of lightning, a lighting up as if of the sun itself, which could burst blocks of rock asunder. The lightning struck and split to the roots the old venerable oak. The crown fell asunder. It seemed as if the tree were stretching forth its arms to clasp the messengers of the light.

No bronze cannon can sound over the land at the birth of a royal child as the thunder sounded at the death of the old oak. The rain streamed down; a refreshing wind was blowing; the storm had gone by, and there was quite a holiday glow on all things. The old clergyman spoke a few words for honorable remembrance, and a painter made a drawing, as a lasting record of the tree.

'Everything passes away,' said the Dryad, 'passes away like a cloud, and never comes back!'

The old clergyman, too, did not come back. The green roof of his school was gone, and his teaching-chair had vanished. The children did not come; but autumn came, and winter came, and then spring also. In all this change of seasons the Dryad looked toward the region where, at night, Paris gleamed with its bright mist far on the horizon.

Forth from the town rushed engine after engine, train after train, whistling and screaming at all hours in the day. In the evening, towards midnight, at daybreak, and all the day through, came the trains. Out of each one, and into each one, streamed people from the country of every king. A new wonder of the world had summoned them to Paris.

In what form did this wonder exhibit itself?

'A splendid blossom of art and industry,' said one, 'has unfolded itself in the Champ de Mars, a gigantic sunflower, from whose petals one can learn geography and statistics, and can become as wise as a lord mayor, and raise one's self to the level of art and poetry, and study the greatness and power of the various lands.'

'A fairy tale flower,' said another, 'a many-colored lotus-plant, which spreads out its green leaves like a velvet carpet over the sand. The opening spring has brought it forth, the summer will see it in all its splendor, the autumn winds will sweep it away, so that not a leaf, not a fragment of its root shall remain.'

In front of the Military School extends in time of peace the arena of war—a field without a blade of grass, a piece of sandy steppe, as if cut out of the Desert of Africa, where Fata Morgana displays her wondrous airy castles and hanging gardens. In the Champ de Mars, however, these were to be seen more splendid, more wonderful than in the East, for human art had converted the airy deceptive scenes into reality.

'The Aladdin's Palace of the present has been built,' it was said. 'Day by day, hour by hour, it unfolds more of its wonderful splendor.'

The endless halls shine in marble and many colors. 'Master Bloodless' here moves his limbs of steel and iron in the great circular hall of machinery. Works of art in metal, in stone, in Gobelins tapestry, announce the vitality of mind that is stirring in every land. Halls of paintings, splendor of flowers, everything that mind and skill can create in the workshop of the artisan, has been placed here for show. Even the memorials of ancient days, out of old graves and turf-moors, have appeared at this general meeting.

The overpowering great variegated whole must be divided into small portions, and pressed together like a plaything, if it is to be understood and described.

Like a great table on Christmas Eve, the Champ de Mars carried a wonder-castle of industry and art, and around this knickknacks from all countries had been ranged, knickknacks on a grand scale, for every nation found some remembrance of home.

Here stood the royal palace of Egypt, there the caravanserai of the desert land. The Bedouin had quitted his sunny country, and hastened by on his camel. Here stood the Russian stables, with the fiery glorious horses of the steppe. Here stood the simple straw-thatched dwelling of the Danish peasant, with the Dannebrog flag, next to Gustavus Vasa's wooden house from Dalarne, with its wonderful carvings. American huts, English cottages, French pavilions, kiosks, theatres, churches, all strewn around, and between them the fresh green turf, the clear springing water, blooming bushes, rare trees, hothouses, in which one might fancy one's self transported into the tropical forest; whole gardens brought from Damascus, and blooming under one roof. What colors, what fragrance!

Artificial grottoes surrounded bodies of fresh or salt water, and gave a glimpse into the empire of the fishes; the visitor seemed to wander at the bottom of the sea, among fishes and polypi.

'All this,' they said, 'the Champ de Mars offers;' and around the great richly-spread table the crowd of human beings moves like a busy swarm of ants, on foot or in little carriages, for not all feet are equal to such a fatiguing journey.

Hither they swarm from morning till late in the evening. Steamer after steamer, crowded with people, glides down the Seine. The number of carriages is continually on the increase. The swarm of people on foot and on horseback grows more and more dense. Carriages and omnibuses are crowded, stuffed and embroidered with people. All these tributary streams flow in one direction—towards the Exhibition. On every entrance the flag of France is displayed; around the world's bazaar wave the flags of all nations. There is a humming and a murmuring from the hall of the machines; from the towers the melody of the chimes is heard; with the tones of the organs in the churches mingle the hoarse nasal songs from the cafes of the East. It is a kingdom of Babel, a wonder of the world!

In very truth it was. That's what all the reports said, and who did not hear them? The Dryad knew everything that is told here of the new wonder in the city of cities.

'Fly away, ye birds! fly away to see, and then come back and tell me,' said the Dryad.

The wish became an intense desire—became the one thought of a life. Then, in the quiet silent night, while the full moon was shining, the Dryad saw a spark fly out of the moon's disc, and fall like a shooting star. And before the tree, whose leaves waved to and fro as if they were stirred by a tempest, stood a noble, mighty, and grand figure. In tones that were at once rich and strong, like the trumpet of the Last Judgment bidding farewell to life and summoning to the great account, it said:

'Thou shalt go to the city of magic; thou shalt take root there, and enjoy the mighty rushing breezes, the air and the sunshine there. But the time of thy life shall then be shortened; the line of years that awaited thee here amid the free nature shall shrink to but a small tale. Poor Dryad! It shall be thy destruction. Thy yearning and longing will increase, thy desire will grow more stormy, the tree itself will be as a prison to thee, thou wilt quit thy cell and give up thy nature to fly out and mingle among men. Then the years that would have belonged to thee will be contracted to half the span of the ephemeral fly, that lives but a day: one night, and thy life-taper shall be blown out—the leaves of the tree will wither and be blown away, to become green never again!'

Thus the words sounded. And the light vanished away, but not the longing of the Dryad. She trembled in the wild fever of expectation.

'I shall go there!' she cried, rejoicingly. 'Life is beginning and swells like a cloud; nobody knows whither it is hastening.'

When the gray dawn arose and the moon turned pale and the clouds were tinted red, the wished-for hour struck. The words of promise were fulfilled.

People appeared with spades and poles; they dug round the roots of the tree, deeper and deeper, and beneath it. A wagon was brought out, drawn by many horses, and the tree was lifted up, with its roots and the lumps of earth that adhered to them; matting was placed around the roots, as though the tree had its feet in a warm bag. And now the tree was lifted on the wagon and secured with chains. The journey began—the journey to

Paris. There the tree was to grow as an ornament to the city of French glory.

The twigs and the leaves of the chestnut tree trembled in the first moments of its being moved; and the Dryad trembled in the pleasurable feeling of expectation.

'Away! away!' it sounded in every beat of her pulse. 'Away! away' sounded in words that flew trembling along. The Dryad forgot to bid farewell to the regions of home; she thought not of the waving grass and of the innocent daisies, which had looked up to her as to a great lady, a young Princess playing at being a shepherdess out in the open air.

The chestnut tree stood upon the wagon, and nodded his branches; whether this meant 'farewell' or 'forward,' the Dryad knew not; she dreamed only of the marvellous new things, that seemed yet so familiar, and that were to unfold themselves before her. No child's heart rejoicing in innocence—no heart whose blood danced with passion—had set out on the journey to Paris more full of expectation than she.

Her 'farewell' sounded in the words 'Away! away!'

The wheels turned; the distant approached; the present vanished. The region was changed, even as the clouds change. New vineyards, forests, villages, villas appeared—came nearer—vanished!

The chestnut tree moved forward, and the Dryad went with it. Steam-engine after steam-engine rushed past, sending up into the air vapory clouds, that formed figures which told of Paris, whence they came, and whither the Dryad was going.

Everything around knew it, and must know whither she was bound. It seemed to her as if every tree she passed stretched out its leaves towards her, with the prayer— "Take me with you! take me with you!" for every tree enclosed a longing Dryad.

What changes during this flight! Houses seemed to be rising out of the earth—more and more—thicker and thicker. The chimneys rose like flower-pots ranged side by side, or in rows one above the other, on the roofs. Great inscriptions in letters a yard long, and figures in various colors, covering the walls from cornice to basement, came brightly out.

'Where does Paris begin, and when shall I be there?' asked the Dryad.

The crowd of people grew; the tumult and the bustle increased; carriage followed upon carriage; people on foot and people on horseback were mingled together; all around were shops on shops, music and song, crying and talking.

The Dryad, in her tree, was now in the midst of Paris. The great heavy wagon all at once stopped on a little square planted with trees. The high houses around had all of them balconies to the windows, from which the inhabitants looked down upon the young fresh chestnut tree, which was coming to be planted here as a substitute for the dead tree that lay stretched on the ground.

The passers-by stood still and smiled in admiration of its pure vernal freshness. The older trees, whose buds were still closed, whispered with their waving branches, 'Welcome! welcome!' The fountain, throwing its jet of water high up in the air, to let it fall again in the wide stone basin, told the wind to sprinkle the new-comer with pearly drops, as if it wished to give him a refreshing draught to welcome him.

The Dryad felt how her tree was being lifted from the wagon to be placed in the spot where it was to stand. The roots were covered with earth, and fresh turf was laid on top. Blooming shrubs and flowers in pots were ranged around; and thus a little garden arose in the square.

The tree that had been killed by the fumes of gas, the steam of kitchens, and the bad air of the city, was put upon the wagon and driven away. The passers-by looked on. Children and old men sat upon the bench, and looked at the green tree. And we who are telling this story stood upon a balcony, and looked down upon the green spring sight that had been brought in from the fresh country air, and said, what the old clergyman would have said, 'Poor Dryad!'

'I am happy! I am happy!' the Dryad cried, rejoicing; 'and yet I cannot realize, cannot describe what I feel. Everything is as I fancied it, and yet as I did not fancy it.'

The houses stood there, so lofty, so close! The sunlight shone on only one of the walls, and that one was stuck over with bills and placards, before which the people stood still; and this made a crowd.

Carriages rushed past, carriages rolled past; light ones and heavy ones mingled together. Omnibuses, those over-crowded moving houses, came rattling by; horsemen galloped among them; even carts and wagons asserted their rights.

The Dryad asked herself if these high-grown houses, which stood so close around her, would not remove and take other shapes, like the clouds in the sky, and draw aside, so that she might cast a glance into Paris, and over it. Notre Dame must show itself, the Vendome Column, and the wondrous building which had called and was still calling so many strangers to the city.

But the houses did not stir from their places. It was yet day when the lamps were lit. The gas-jets gleamed from the shops, and shone even into the branches of the trees, so that it was like sunlight in summer. The stars above made their appearance, the same to which the Dryad had looked up in her home. She thought she felt a clear pure stream of air which went forth from them. She felt herself lifted up and strengthened, and felt an increased power of seeing through every leaf and through every fibre of the root. Amid all the noise and the turmoil, the colors and the lights, she knew herself watched by mild eyes.

From the side streets sounded the merry notes of fiddles and wind instruments. Up! to the dance, to the dance! to jollity and pleasure! that was their invitation. Such music it was, that horses, carriages, trees, and houses would have danced, if they had known how. The charm of intoxicating delight filled the bosom of the Dryad.

'How glorious, how splendid it is!' she cried, rejoicingly. 'Now I am in Paris!'

The next day that dawned, the next night that fell, offered the same spectacle, similar bustle, similar life; changing, indeed, yet always the same; and thus it went on through the sequence of days.

'Now I know every tree, every flower on the square here! I know every house, every balcony, every shop in this narrow cut-off corner, where I am denied the sight of this great mighty city. Where are the arches of triumph, the Boulevards, the wondrous building of the world? I see nothing of all this. As if shut up in a cage, I stand among the high houses, which I now know by heart, with their inscriptions, signs, and placards; all the painted confectionery, that is no longer to my taste. Where are all the things of which I heard, for which I longed, and for whose sake I wanted to come hither? what have I seized, found, won? I feel the same longing I felt before; I feel that there is a life I should wish to grasp and to experience. I must go out into the ranks of living men, and mingle among them. I must fly about like a bird. I must see and feel, and become human altogether. I must enjoy the one half-day, instead of vegetating for years in every-day sameness and weariness, in which I become ill, and at last sink and disappear like the dew on the meadows. I will gleam like the cloud, gleam in the sunshine of life, look out over the whole like the cloud, and pass away like it, no one knoweth whither.'

Thus sighed the Dryad; and she prayed:

'Take from me the years that were destined for me, and give me but half of the life of the ephemeral fly!

Deliver me from my prison! Give me human life, human happiness, only a short span, only the one night, if it cannot be otherwise; and then punish me for my wish to live, my longing for life! Strike me out of thy list. Let my shell, the fresh young tree, wither, or be hewn down, and burnt to ashes, and scattered to all the winds!'

A rustling went through the leaves of the tree; there was a trembling in each of the leaves; it seemed as if fire streamed through it. A gust of wind shook its green crown, and from the midst of that crown a female figure came forth. In the same moment she was sitting beneath the brightly-illuminated leafy branches, young and beautiful to behold, like poor Mary, to whom the clergyman had said, 'The great city will be thy destruction.'

The Dryad sat at the foot of the tree—at her house door, which she had locked, and whose key had thrown away. So young! so fair! The stars saw her, and blinked at her. The gas-lamps saw her, and gleamed and beckoned to her. How delicate she was, and yet how blooming!—a child, and yet a grown maiden! Her dress was fine as silk, green as the freshly-opened leaves on the crown of the tree; in her nut-brown hair clung a half-opened chestnut blossom. She looked like the Goddess of Spring.

For one short minute she sat motionless; then she sprang up, and, light as a gazelle, she hurried away. She ran and sprang like the reflection from the mirror that, carried by the sunshine, is cast, now here, now there. Could any one have followed her with his eyes, he would have seen how marvellously her dress and her form changed, according to the nature of the house or the place whose light happened to shine upon her.

She reached the Boulevards. Here a sea of light streamed forth from the gas-flames of the lamps, the shops and the cafes. Here stood in a row young and slender trees, each of which concealed its Dryad, and gave shade from the artificial sunlight. The whole vast pavement was one great festive hall, where covered tables stood laden with refreshments of all kinds, from champagne and Chartreuse down to coffee and beer. Here was an exhibition of flowers, statues, books, and colored stuffs.

From the crowd close by the lofty houses she looked forth over the terrific stream beyond the rows of trees. Yonder heaved a stream of rolling carriages, cabriolets, coaches, omnibuses, cabs, and among them riding gentlemen and marching troops. To cross to the opposite shore was an undertaking fraught with danger to life and limb. Now lanterns shed their radiance abroad; now the gas had the upper hand; suddenly a rocket rises! Whence? Whither?

Here are sounds of soft Italian melodies; yonder, Spanish songs are sung, accompanied by the rattle of the castanets; but strongest of all, and predominating over the rest, the street-organ tunes of the moment, the exciting 'Can-Can' music, which Orpheus never knew, and which was never heard by the 'Belle Helene.' Even the barrow was tempted to hop upon one of its wheels.

The Dryad danced, floated, flew, changing her color every moment, like a humming-bird in the sunshine;

each house, with the world belonging to it, gave her its own reflections.

As the glowing lotus-flower, torn from its stem, is carried away by the stream, so the Dryad drifted along. Whenever she paused, she was another being, so that none was able to follow her, to recognize her, or to look more closely at her.

Like cloud-pictures, all things flew by her. She looked into a thousand faces, but not one was familiar to her; she saw not a single form from home. Two bright eyes had remained in her memory. She thought of Mary, poor Mary, the ragged merry child, who wore the red flowers in her black hair. Mary was now here, in the world-city, rich and magnificent as in that day when she drove past the house of the old clergyman, and past the tree of the Dryad, the old oak.

Here she was certainly living, in the deafening tumult. Perhaps she had just stepped out of one of the gorgeous carriages in waiting. Handsome equipages, with coachmen in gold braid and footmen in silken hose, drove up. The people who alighted from them were all richly-dressed ladies. They went through the opened gate, and ascended the broad staircase that led to a building resting on marble pillars. Was this building, perhaps, the wonder of the world? There Mary would certainly be found.

'Sancta Maria!' resounded from the interior. Incense floated through the lofty painted and gilded aisles, where a solemn twilight reigned.

It was the Church of the Madeleine.

Clad in black garments of the most costly stuffs, fashioned according to the latest mode, the rich feminine world of Paris glided across the shining pavement. The crests of the proprietors were engraved on silver shields on the velvet-bound prayer-books, and embroidered in the corners of perfumed handkerchiefs bordered with Brussels lace. A few of the ladies were kneeling in silent prayer before the altars; others resorted to the confessionals.

Anxiety and fear took possession of the Dryad; she felt as if she had entered a place where she had no right to be. Here was the abode of silence, the hall of secrets. Everything was said in whispers, every word was a mystery.

The Dryad saw herself enveloped in lace and silk, like the women of wealth and of high birth around her. Had, perhaps, every one of them a longing in her breast, like the Dryad?

A deep, painful sigh was heard. Did it escape from some confessional in a distant corner, or from the bosom of the Dryad? She drew the veil closer around her; she breathed incense, and not the fresh air. Here was not the abiding-place of her longing.

Away! away—a hastening without rest. The ephemeral fly knows not repose, for her existence is flight.

She was out again among the gas candelabra, by a magnificent fountain.

'All its streaming waters are not able to wash out the innocent blood that was spilt here.'

Such were the words spoken. Strangers stood around, carrying on a lively conversation, such as no one would have dared to carry on in the gorgeous hall of secrets whence the Dryad came.

A heavy stone slab was turned and then lifted. She did not understand why. She saw an opening that led into the depths below. The strangers stepped down, leaving the starlit air and the cheerful life of the upper world behind them.

'I am afraid,' said one of the women who stood around, to her husband, 'I cannot venture to go down, nor do I care for the wonders down yonder. You had better stay here with me.'

'Indeed, and travel home,' said the man, 'and quit Paris without having seen the most wonderful thing of all—the real wonder of the present period, created by the power and resolution of one man!'

'I will not go down for all that,' was the reply.

'The wonder of the present time,' it had been called. The Dryad had heard and had understood it. The goal of her ardent longing had thus been reached, and here was the entrance to it. Down into the depths below Paris? She had not thought of such a thing; but now she heard it said, and saw the strangers descending, and went after them.

The staircase was of cast iron, spiral, broad and easy. Below there burned a lamp, and farther down, another. They stood in a labyrinth of endless halls and arched passages, all communicating with each other. All the streets and lanes of Paris were to be seen here again, as in a dim reflection. The names were painted up; and every house above had its number down here also, and struck its roots under the macadamized quays of a broad canal, in which the muddy water flowed onward. Over it the fresh streaming water was carried on arches; and quite at the top hung the tangled net of gas-pipes and telegraph-wires.

In the distance lamps gleamed, like a reflection from the world-city above. Every now and then a dull rumbling was heard. This came from the heavy wagons rolling over the entrance bridges.

Whither had the Dryad come?

You have, no doubt, heard of the CATACOMBS? Now they are vanishing points in that new underground world—that wonder of the present day—the sewers of Paris. The Dryad was there, and not in the world's Exhibition in the Champ de Mars.

She heard exclamations of wonder and admiration.

'From here go forth health and life for thousands upon thousands up yonder! Our time is the time of progress, with its manifold blessings.'

Such was the opinion and the speech of men; but not of those creatures who had been born here, and who built and dwelt here—of the rats, namely, who were squeaking to one another in the clefts of a crumbling wall, quite plainly, and in a way the Dryad understood well.

A big old Father-Rat, with his tail bitten off, was relieving his feelings in loud squeaks; and his family gave their tribute of concurrence to every word he said:

'I am disgusted with this man-mewing,' he cried—'with these outbursts of ignorance. A fine magnificence, truly! all made up of gas and petroleum! I can't eat such stuff as that. Everything here is so fine and bright now, that one's ashamed of one's self, without exactly knowing why. Ah, if we only lived in the days of tallow candles! and it does not lie so very far behind us. That was a romantic time, as one may say.'

'What are you talking of there?' asked the Dryad. 'I have never seen you before. What is it you are talking about?'

'Of the glorious days that are gone,' said the Rat—'of the happy time of our great-grandfathers and great-grandmothers. Then it was a great thing to get down here. That was a rat's nest quite different from Paris. Mother Plague used to live here then; she killed people, but never rats. Robbers and smugglers could breathe freely here. Here was the meeting-place of the most interesting personages, whom one now only gets to see in the theatres where they act melodrama, up above. The time of romance is gone even in our rat's nest; and here also fresh air and petroleum have broken in.'

Thus squeaked the Rat; he squeaked in honor of the old time, when Mother Plague was still alive.

A carriage stopped, a kind of open omnibus, drawn by swift horses. The company mounted and drove away along the Boulevard de Sebastopol, that is to say, the underground boulevard, over which the well-known crowded street of that name extended.

The carriage disappeared in the twilight; the Dryad disappeared, lifted to the cheerful freshness above. Here, and not below in the vaulted passages, filled with heavy air, the wonder work must be found which she was to seek in her short lifetime. It must gleam brighter than all the gas-flames, stronger than the moon that was just gliding past.

Yes, certainly, she saw it yonder in the distance, it gleamed before her, and twinkled and glittered like the evening star in the sky.

She saw a glittering portal open, that led to a little garden, where all was brightness and dance music. Colored lamps surrounded little lakes, in which were water-plants of colored metal, from whose flowers jets of water spurted up. Beautiful weeping willows, real products of spring, hung their fresh branches over these lakes like a fresh, green, transparent, and yet screening veil. In the bushes burnt an open fire, throwing a red twilight over the quiet huts of branches, into which the sounds of music penetrated—an ear tickling, intoxicating music, that sent the blood coursing through the veins.

Beautiful girls in festive attire, with pleasant smiles on their lips, and the light spirit of youth in their hearts—'Marys,' with roses in their hair, but without carriage and postilion—flitted to and fro in the wild dance.

Where were the heads, where the feet? As if stung by tarantulas, they sprang, laughed, rejoiced, as if in their ecstacies they were going to embrace all the world.

The Dryad felt herself torn with them into the whirl of the dance. Round her delicate foot clung the silken boot, chestnut brown in color, like the ribbon that floated from her hair down upon her bare shoulders. The green silk dress waved in large folds, but did not entirely hide the pretty foot and ankle.

Had she come to the enchanted Garden of Armida? What was the name of the place?

The name glittered in gas-jets over the entrance. It was 'Mabille.'

The soaring upwards of rockets, the splashing of fountains, and the popping of champagne corks accompanied the wild bacchantic dance. Over the whole glided the moon through the air, clear, but with a somewhat crooked face.

A wild joviality seemed to rush through the Dryad, as though she were intoxicated with opium. Her eyes spoke, her lips spoke, but the sound of violins and of flutes drowned the sound of her voice. Her partner whispered words to her which she did not understand, nor do we understand them. He stretched out his arms to draw her to him, but he embraced only the empty air.

The Dryad had been carried away, like a rose-leaf on the wind. Before her she saw a flame in the air, a flashing light high up on a tower. The beacon light shone from the goal of her longing, shone from the red lighthouse tower of the Fata Morgana of the Champ de Mars. Thither she was carried by the wind. She circled round the tower; the workmen thought it was a butterfly that had come too early, and that now sank down dying.

The moon shone bright, gas-lamps spread light around, through the halls, over the all-world's buildings scattered about, over the rose-hills and the rocks produced by human ingenuity, from which waterfalls, driven by the power of 'Master Bloodless,' fell down. The caverns of the sea, the depths of the lakes, the kingdom of the fishes were opened here. Men walked as in the depths of the deep pond, and held converse with the sea, in the diving-bell of glass. The water pressed against the strong glass walls above and on every side. The polypi, eel-like living creatures, had fastened themselves to the bottom, and stretched out arms, fathoms long, for prey. A big turbot was making himself broad in front, quietly enough, but not without casting some suspicious glances aside. A crab clambered over him, looking like a gigantic spider, while the shrimps wandered about in restless haste, like the butterflies and moths of the sea.

In the fresh water grew water-lilies, nymphaea, and reeds; the gold-fishes stood up below in rank and file, all turning their heads one way, that the streaming water might flow into their mouths. Fat carps stared at the glass wall with stupid eyes. They knew that they were here to be exhibited, and that they had made the somewhat toilsome journey hither in tubs filled with water; and they thought with dismay of the land-sickness from which they had suffered so cruelly on the railway.

They had come to see the Exhibition, and now contemplated it from their fresh or salt-water position. They looked attentively at the crowds of people who passed by them early and late. All the nations in the world, they thought, had made an exhibition of their inhabitants, for the edification of the soles and haddocks, pike and carp, that they might give their opinions upon the different kinds.

'Those are scaly animals,' said a little slimy Whiting. 'They put on different scales two or three times a day, and they emit sounds which they call speaking. We don't put on scales, and we make ourselves understood in an easier way, simply by twitching the corners of our mouths and staring with our eyes. We have a great many advantages over mankind.'

'But they have learned swimming of us,' remarked a well-educated Codling. 'You must know I come from the great sea outside. In the hot time of the year the people yonder go into the water; first they take off their scales, and then they swim. They have learnt from the frogs to kick out with their hind legs, and row with their fore paws. But they cannot hold out long. They want to be like us, but they cannot come up to us. Poor people!'

And the fishes stared. They thought that the whole swarm of people whom they had seen in the bright daylight were still moving around them; they were certain they still saw the same forms that had first caught their attention.

A pretty Barbel, with spotted skin, and an enviably round back, declared that the 'human fry' were still there.

'I can see a well set-up human figure quite well,' said the Barbel. 'She was called 'contumacious lady,' or something of that kind. She had a mouth and staring eyes, like ours, and a great balloon at the back of her head, and something like a shut-up umbrella in front; there were a lot of dangling bits of seaweed hanging about her. She ought to take all the rubbish off, and go as we do; then she would look something like a respectable barbel, so far as it is possible for a person to look like one!'

'What's become of that one whom they drew away with the hook? He sat on a wheel-chair, and had paper, and pen, and ink, and wrote down everything. They called him a 'writer.'

'They're going about with him still,' said a hoary old maid of a Carp, who carried her misfortune about with her, so that she was quite hoarse. In her youth she had once swallowed a hook, and still swam patiently about with it in her gullet. 'A writer? That means, as we fishes describe it, a kind of cuttle or ink-fish among men.'

Thus the fishes gossipped in their own way; but in the artificial water-grotto the laborers were busy; who were obliged to take advantage of the hours of night to get their work done by daybreak. They accompanied with blows of their hammers and with songs the parting words of the vanishing Dryad.

'So, at any rate, I have seen you, you pretty gold-fishes,' she said. 'Yes, I know you;' and she waved her hand to them. 'I have known about you a long time in my home; the swallow told me about you. How beautiful you are! how delicate and shining! I should like to kiss every one of you. You others, also. I know you all; but you do not know me.'

The fishes stared out into the twilight. They did not understand a word of it.

The Dryad was there no longer. She had been a long time in the open air, where the different countries—the country of black bread, the codfish coast, the kingdom of Russia leather, and the banks of eau-de-Cologne, and the gardens of rose oil—exhaled their perfumes from the world-wonder flower.

When, after a night at a ball, we drive home half asleep and half awake, the melodies still sound plainly in our ears; we hear them, and could sing them all from memory. When the eye of the murdered man closes, the picture of what it saw last clings to it for a time like a photographic picture.

So it was likewise here. The bustling life of day had not yet disappeared in the quiet night. The Dryad had seen it; she knew, thus it will be repeated tomorrow.

The Dryad stood among the fragrant roses, and thought she knew them, and had seen them in her own home. She also saw red pomegranate flowers, like those that little Mary had worn in her dark hair.

Remembrances from the home of her childhood flashed through her thoughts; her eyes eagerly drank in the prospect around, and feverish restlessness chased her through the wonder-filled halls.

A weariness that increased continually, took possession of her. She felt a longing to rest on the soft Oriental carpets within, or to lean against the weeping willow without by the clear water. But for the ephemeral fly there was no rest. In a few moments the day had completed its circle.

Her thoughts trembled, her limbs trembled, she sank down on the grass by the bubbling water.

'Thou wilt ever spring living from the earth,' she said mournfully. 'Moisten my tongue—bring me a refreshing draught.'

'I am no living water,' was the answer. 'I only spring upward when the machine wills it.'

'Give me something of thy freshness, thou green grass,' implored the Dryad; 'give me one of thy fragrant flowers.'

'We must die if we are torn from our stalks,' replied the Flowers and the Grass.

'Give me a kiss, thou fresh stream of air—only a single life-kiss.'

'Soon the sun will kiss the clouds red,' answered the Wind; 'then thou wilt be among the dead—blown away, as all the splendor here will be blown away before the year shall have ended. Then I can play again with the light loose sand on the place here, and whirl the dust over the land and through the air. All is dust!'

The Dryad felt a terror like a woman who has cut asunder her pulse-artery in the bath, but is filled again with the love of life, even while she is bleeding to death. She raised herself, tottered forward a few steps, and sank down again at the entrance to a little church. The gate stood open, lights were burning upon the altar, and the organ sounded.

What music! Such notes the Dryad had never yet heard; and yet it seemed to her as if she recognised a number of well-known voices among them. They came deep from the heart of all creation. She thought she heard the stories of the old clergyman, of great deeds, and of the celebrated names, and of the gifts that the creatures of God must bestow upon posterity, if they would live on in the world.

The tones of the organ swelled, and in their song there sounded these words:

'Thy wishing and thy longing have torn thee, with thy roots, from the place which God appointed for thee. That was thy destruction, thou poor Dryad!'

The notes became soft and gentle, and seemed to die away in a wail.

In the sky the clouds showed themselves with a ruddy gleam. The Wind sighed:

'Pass away, ye dead! now the sun is going to rise!'

The first ray fell on the Dryad. Her form was irradiated in changing colors, like the soap-bubble when it is bursting and becomes a drop of water; like a tear that falls and passes away like a vapor.

Poor Dryad! Only a dew-drop, only a tear, poured upon the earth, and vanished away!